A FATHER'S PROMISE

DONNALYNN HESS

JOURNEYFORTH

Greenville, South Carolina

A Father's Promise

Edited by Michael Garrett Deas
Cover design by Jamie Miller
Illustrations by Stephanie True

Photo credits for pages 251–58
1. National Archives (Worldwide Photos)
2. National Archives
3. National Archives
4. National Archives
5. National Archives
6. National Archives (Heinrich Hoffman)
7. National Archives (Heinrich Hoffman)
8. National Archives (Heinrich Hoffman)
9. National Archives (Heinrich Hoffman)
10. National Archives
11. National Archives
12. National Archives
13. National Archives

© 1987 by BJU Press
Greenville, SC 29614
JourneyForth Books is a division of BJU Press

Printed in the United States of America

ISBN 978-0-89084-379-6

20   19

CONTENTS

PART TWO: Child of the Forest

Photo section follows page 250

to my teacher

He that dwelleth in the secret place of the most High shall abide under the shadow of the Almighty.

PROLOGUE

But the God of all grace, who hath called us unto his eternal glory by Christ Jesus, after that ye have suffered a while, make you perfect, stablish, strengthen, settle you.
—I Peter 5:10

In the secret place of every young boy's heart there is a desire to be a hero. It is a desire that grows as he grows, if he is growing as God intended. But the road that takes a boy from dreams of heroism to true acts of manly courage is not easily traveled. It is often a hard road—a road hedged in with the thorns of adversity and strewn with the blood-red flowers of sorrow. Eleven-year-old Rudi Kaplan, the hero of this story, must travel such a road. But he takes with him on his journey the promise of God, a promise given to him by his father.

His journey begins in 1939 at the outset of World War II. At this time Rudi lives with his father, Jakob Kaplan, in Warsaw, Poland. Dr. Kaplan is a Polish Jew, but he is also a Christian. He accepted Christ while studying to be a doctor at a university in Stockholm, Sweden. It was also in Sweden that Rudi's father and mother met and married. They returned to Warsaw a year after Rudi was born. But soon after their return, they learned that Mrs. Kaplan was dying. Rudi was only three when his mother went to be with the Lord.

1

Rudi's heritage plays an important role during this time in his life. From his father he inherits his Jewish blood; from his mother, his Swedish appearance. Both prove significant: the first is to set him on the road to heroism; the second, to protect him on the journey.

Return of the
of the
Tartars

CHAPTER ONE
THE TRUMPETER'S SONG
SEPT. 1939

*Yea, a sword shall pierce through thy own soul also,
that the thoughts of many hearts may be revealed.*
                                                    —Luke 2:35

When Rudi stepped out into the sunlight, a cool
September wind swept over him. He stood a moment,
feeling the wind against his face and listening to the rumble
of the morning trolley and the clatter of the horse-drawn
carriages.

"Good morning, Rudi," said Mr. Kaminsky as he came
out of their apartment building.

"Morning," Rudi said.

"How's your father?" he asked as he hurried out into
the street.

"Fine," Rudi called after him.

Mr. Kaminsky's usual morning greeting seemed to
reassure Rudi that this day would be as any other. And
throwing his book bag over his shoulder, he set out to
meet his best friend, Salek Serdusek.

"Have you heard what's happened to the German
Jews?" Salek asked as soon as they had met.

Rudi tried to sound nonchalant. "No—what?"

"The Nazis are attacking them in the streets, and the police are playing blind. There was an awful riot last night in Berlin!"

"Where'd you hear that?" asked Rudi.

"Radio. Papa says if Hitler gets to Warsaw, we're as good as dead."

"He won't get that far."

"I hope you're right," Salek said thoughtfully. "But if they do," he added, "papa also said that you and your father would stand a better chance than we would."

"What made him say a thing like that?" asked Rudi.

" 'Cause even though you're Jews, you believe like they do."

"Like who?" Rudi demanded.

"Like the Germans," Salek told him.

"We don't 'believe' like the Germans," said Rudi defensively.

"He just meant you believe in their Messiah. You know—you're a Christian."

"Hitler's no Christian."

"Well, he's no Jew," Salek countered. "Besides, he says he's a Christian. Says that's why he hates the Jews."

"I don't care what he says, he's not. And you know it!"

"Don't get riled," said Salek. "Papa wouldn't say anything against you or your father—especially your father. They've been friends for too long. Like you and me. And I must admit," he continued in a lighter tone, "now that I think about it, you and Hitler don't seem to have much in common."

"No," said Rudi, relieved at the change in mood. "But now that I think about it, I'd say you and he are alike in at least two ways."

"Yeah? How?"

"You're both short and funny-looking." He burst out laughing and took off down the street with Salek at his heels.

By the time the two boys parted at their usual corner, thoughts of war had all but disappeared from Rudi's mind. As he continued on alone, he thought how much better it would be if he and Salek could attend school together. Rudi had plenty of friends at school, but none of them were like Salek.

Rudi never really understood why Salek's father had insisted that Salek attend a Jewish school. Mr. Serdusek hardly seemed concerned with religion. Rudi even heard him say once that he attended the synagogue every Sabbath not because God commanded it but because his clients expected it.

God was also the one subject that Mr. Serdusek refused to discuss at length with Rudi's father. Rudi had often listened to them talk for hours about medicine, law, politics, and business, but as soon as Rudi's father brought God into the discussion, Mr. Serdusek would brush the subject aside. Still, Rudi and his father would continue to pray. *And perhaps someday,* Rudi thought, *Mr. Serdusek will listen. And once he listens, Salek will listen too.*

As Rudi neared his classroom, he was surprised to hear the clear, rich sound of a trumpet playing. He recognized the music. It was the trumpeter's song, a song played every hour by the watchman of a famous church in Krakow.

Rudi entered the room quietly and took his seat, for he could see that none of his classmates were engaged in their usual before-school chatter. Instead, everyone, including his teacher, was listening to one of the boys in the class as he played the solemn tune.

As soon as the boy had finished, the teacher rose to address the class. "You all know that Hitler's troops have marched into Poland," she began. "You know too that our soldiers are doing all that they can to stop his advance, and we can help them by building barricades and digging trenches to protect our city. For this reason, the authorities thought it best if school were dismissed—indefinitely."

Rudi looked around at his classmates. Everyone seemed stunned.

"But before I let you go, I want to read a story, one I had planned for beginning today's lessons. I arranged for us to listen to the 'Heynal,' or trumpeter's song, because I thought it would be a good way to introduce the story. I'm sure that most of you are familiar with the music. You may not remember, however, why it is so famous. I think that today is a good day for us to remember." With this introduction, she opened an old but well-kept book and began to read.

The Tartars were marching once again—and they were marching toward Krakow. The news made even the brawniest peasant tremble and the women and children weep, because the Poles knew the Tartars to be a fierce, unfeeling people. It was never difficult to follow their path. You knew the direction they were heading by the hordes of refugees fleeing from them. And the charred earth and desolate houses always signified where they had been.

So it was in the spring of 1241. The young trumpeter of Krakow was keeping watch high in the church tower when he saw a procession of terrified villagers on the outskirts of the city. They were on foot, not far from the city's entrance. The women were hurrying the children along while the men clasped their weapons and glanced behind them. At first the boy did not grasp what was happening. Then he looked past the peasants and saw mounds of dust rising from the dry earth. Tartar horses were carrying their vicious masters full speed toward the city.

Hurriedly he gave a signal, and the gates were opened long enough for the refugees to enter. The sound of rearing horses mingled with cries of fury confirmed that the entry had been barred again not a moment too soon. But barred gates offered only temporary protection against such an enemy.

By nightfall the Tartars had prepared battering rams, and before long the gates' massive beams began to crack and groan under the force of their blows. The leaders of the city decided to move as many people as they could into the central castle. It was the only stronghold they felt sure the enemy could not conquer.

When the young trumpeter saw the people making their way to the fortress, he took up his trumpet and turned to descend the tower. But as he did, the words of the trumpeter's oath came back to him. "I swear on my honor as a Pole that I will faithfully unto death, if need be, sound upon the trumpet the 'Heynal' each hour in the tower of the church." *Unto death*—the words struck with new force. When he had first taken the oath, he had thought the words sounded grand and patriotic; but being a boy, he had never let them sink into his heart—until now.

For over a year he had been faithful to his duty. Every hour he had played his song, and the townspeople always said that his music was much like the song of birds in spring; it gave them the feeling that all was as it should be. He stood for several moments, turning the words of the oath over and over in his mind. Then he sat down against the tower wall, fixed his eyes on the hourglass, and determined to wait for the hour to pass.

His resolution weakened as he heard the gates give way and listened to the savage cries of brutal men pillaging the city. He grew calmer, however, when he remembered that his family was safe within the castle, and that even in the castle they would hear his music. They would know he had kept his promise—that he had not failed the people or the king.

The last grains of sand dropped to the bottom of the hourglass as he rose and moved to the window. He stood a moment, watching the flames leaping up from the deserted houses and unguarded buildings. *They have not conquered the Poles,* he thought, *only a deserted Polish city.* With this thought he raised the trumpet to his lips.

The clear, strong music could be heard even above the invaders' tumult. In a rage the enemy warriors looked about, trying to find the one who dared rise up and defy their victory. They spied the boy and dispatched an arrow. It pierced his heart, breaking off his music—but not his song. For the song still lives in the heart of every noble Polish patriot.

Let it live in our hearts as well," Rudi's teacher said as she closed the book. Then with a nod, she dismissed the class. They left in silence.

As Rudi turned again toward home, he noticed that a change had come over the city. People now hurried through the streets, darting in and out of shops. Some were already busy building barricades. Still others were mounting horses—shovels in hand—and galloping off to help those digging trenches on the outskirts of the city.

He looked up, half expecting to see the trumpeter peering out of one of the cathedral windows. Instead he saw birds flying frantically from building to building. They were afraid to light, for the rooftops of cathedrals were now haunted by men and their machine guns.

CHAPTER TWO
THE AWAKENING
SEPT. 1939

And ye shall hear of wars and rumours of wars.
—Matthew 24:6a

The fears that Rudi could conquer in the daylight were not so easily mastered in the night. How could he fight against fears that came upon him in his sleep? It was as if he had been attacked from behind and dealt a blow that sent him sprawling.

For several minutes after he had awakened, he wrestled with himself until he could stand it no longer and lighted the lamp beside his bed. The light, however, gave him no comfort, for it made him feel cowardly. Angry at his weakness, he flung the covers from him.

The floor felt cool beneath his feet as he got up and moved to his window. From his upper room he could see much of the city, and the view always made him feel as if he were sitting atop the world. He opened the window and breathed in the cool night air. As he did, he noticed that his was not the only lighted room in Warsaw. Perhaps the news of war had awakened not just schoolboys but also grown men and women from their sleep. Perhaps he was not such a coward after all.

He looked past the lighted rooms to the museums, libraries, cathedrals, and palaces outlined in the moonlight—solid, sturdy buildings that had been there hundreds of years. Their whirling spirals, stained glass, and intricately carved decorations rose up before him to defy his feelings of uncertainty, and he took comfort in looking on those things which he thought could never change.

His eyes eventually came to rest on one cathedral. He then thought back to the first moment he had noticed it. It was on his seventh birthday, the day that he received his mother's first letter. When Rudi's mother had found out that she was dying, Rudi was too young to store up memories of her. So she had decided to write as many letters to him as she could. He had already received five of the seven that she had completed.

He went to his desk and brought out the old wooden box where he kept her letters. Rummaging through the box, he located the one dated November 15, 1934. It was in this one that the reason for his interest in the dark and curiously structured building was found. He then returned to the window, settled himself comfortably on the ledge, and began to read.

for Nov. 15, 1934

Dear Rudi,

This is just one of many birthday letters you will receive from me. Your father will give you this one on your seventh birthday, since I want you to begin receiving them when you can read them for yourself. Of course, he will have to help you with this first one, as he will have to help you through the years with many "first-time" things. But he won't mind. You will find, as I have found, that he is a very patient man. I will tell you more of what I know of him in later letters. For now let me

simply tell you why I decided I would write. Obviously, one reason is to wish you HAPPY BIRTHDAY!

A second reason is to share with you some of the family memories that have meant so much to me—like the memory of the day you were born. When your father saw you, he looked at me and said, "Ingrid, you should have told me that our son would look more like a Swede than a Jew."

"Why," I said, a little offended, "I am a Swede, and you never seemed to mind my looks."

He tried to look serious. "Don't you understand," he said, "how hard it is for a Swede to grow a decent beard?"

By then I could see that there was laughter in his eyes, and I replied, "I should say that what grows in his heart will be more important than what grows on his chin."

He laughed a deep, contented laugh, and then he took you in his arms. "If he has your wit and my stature," he said, "he will not need a beard!" And with each passing day he grew more proud of his "Swedish" son.

The third—and most important—reason I am writing is to let you know how much I love you, and how much I wish that I could be with you as you grow. You see, I am hoping that these letters can in some measure take the place of bedtime stories, birthday parties, and bandaged knees. That they will say to you those everyday "I love you's" that I will not be there to say.

One more thing before I close this letter. I'm sitting in your room in front of the window as I write. I love this view. When we moved into this apartment, I thought that there would come a time when you and I would sit here together. We would look out over the city at all the fascinating buildings, and make up adventure stories about them to entertain each other. Since the Lord has seen fit to change my plans, I would like for you to do me a favor. After you have finished celebrating, go up to your room, look out the window, and write a story for me. When you are ready for bed tonight, you can sit before the window and read it to your father. I'm sure that your story will be a good way to end what I hope will be a very happy day.

Love,
Mother

She was right. It was a good way to end a birthday. His father had been so proud of the adventure story that his praise for Rudi was unbounded. It was Rudi's first clear remembrance of making someone really proud of him, and he never forgot how good the feeling was.

Rudi turned again to the cathedral that had sparked his imagination. It still reminded him of an old castle. In his story this "castle" had been guarded by a hooded man who allowed no one to see his face. Those who had been unfortunate enough to catch a glimpse of him had either died or were taken captive. The writing of his story ended there, but the story did not. The next day when he told it to Salek, they spent hours devising plans to rescue the prisoners from the darkened mansion.

Through the years he and Salek had enhanced and revised the story, but one thing remained the same. They were always brave, always successful in their attempts to overcome the strong but evil guard. As Rudi thought about the story, he realized that for the first time it failed to give him pleasure. And as he put away his mother's letter, closed the window, and returned to his bed, he wondered if he would ever imagine another rescue. He wondered if, even in his dreaming, he could ever feel really brave again.

CHAPTER THREE
BLITZKRIEG!
SEPT. 1939

It is of the Lord's mercies that we are not consumed.
—Lamentations 3:22a

By 6:00 the next morning Rudi and his father were already on their way to meet Salek and Mr. Serdusek. They were to join them at the edge of town to dig trenches. When they arrived, Salek and his father were already waiting.

"I think we can work right over here," Mr. Serdusek said. "Looks like somebody started digging and left."

"Fine." Rudi's father jumped down into the half-completed trench.

"What should Salek and I do?" asked Rudi as he followed his father's lead and slid down into the hole.

"I think it would be best for you two boys to take the small picks and loosen the dirt," his father said. "Then we can use the shovels to heave it out of the ditch."

"Let's get at it then," said Mr. Serdusek. "The farmers will be back soon."

"They're collecting the dirt into feedbags and carrying it on carts into the city," Salek told Rudi. "They're using it for barricades. They've already taken one load."

Mr. Serdusek handed Salek a pick. "Let's not keep them waiting for the second," he said.

Since Jakob Kaplan was a doctor and Eryk Serdusek a lawyer, neither of them was used to hour after hour of such manual labor. Nor were their boys. But despite aching muscles and blistered hands, they kept up a steady pace for the better part of the morning.

"What time is it, papa?" Rudi finally asked.

"Ten o'clock."

"Just think," said Salek, "if things were normal, we'd be in school right now. And though I never thought I'd say this, I wish we were."

"Me too," Rudi replied.

"That's nothing." Salek teased him. "You never did mind school as much as I did."

"Maybe not, but I bet I mind digging as much as you do!" Rudi said.

"We'd be done in half the time if you boys did your share," snapped Mr. Serdusek.

"Papa, we're doing our share," Salek said.

Rudi was just about to second Salek's point when he caught his father's eye and thought better of it. But though he managed to control his tongue, he was less successful in mastering his thoughts. *What a difference between Salek's papa and mine,* he said to himself. *As if things aren't bad enough without his grousing.* He turned to glance at Salek, who was staring up at Mr. Serdusek. There was something in Salek's expression, something sad and pleading that Rudi could not quite understand. Still, as he looked at his friend, his anger faded.

"Rudi." Rudi turned from Salek to his father. "Why don't you take a few minutes and rest, son."

"You might as well take a break too, Salek," Mr. Serdusek said in a kinder tone. Then he added, "Maybe after resting you can do better."

Salek kept on digging. "I'm fine."

Rudi took his father's advice and settled himself down in the trench. As he did, he noticed how deep it was getting. The top of it now came to his father's chest. Dr. Kaplan was lean and unusually tall. But in spite of his stature he possessed a certain grace, and as Rudi watched his father's steady movements, his thoughts began to drift. The next thing he knew, Mr. Serdusek was shouting.

"I tell you, if Hitler enters Warsaw, we are dead men!"

"We are not conquered yet," Rudi's father answered.

"You are no fool, Jakob. You know the truth. It has been only a week, and already the Polish infantry has been crushed between the iron jaws of Hitler's army! Every day more refugees pour into the city. I tell you, it can't be long before the Germans stand at the very gates."

"That's why we're here- to provide a way to protect ourselves if that should happen. Besides, the English and French have kept their word and have declared war on Germany. They will do what they can to save Poland."

"They may come to the aid of the Gentiles—but not the Jews! If Jews are to be saved, we will have to save ourselves!"

By this time, Mr. Serdusek had stopped digging and had pushed his shovel deep into the earth. Both Rudi and Salek looked up. Dr. Kaplan kept up his determined pace and said nothing.

"I know what you are thinking!" Mr. Serdusek said. "You think that they will spare you because you are a follower of their Christ!"

Rudi's father now stood upright. His features looked strangely rigid. Salek went back to work, digging more vigorously. But Rudi sat wide-eyed, openly staring at the two men.

"You know as well as I that those who follow Hitler do not follow Christ," Rudi's father countered. "That scoundrel sees himself as a messiah—he knows nothing of my Saviour!"

Rudi had never seen his father's fury; neither had Eryk Serdusek. He drew back as if surprised not only by his friend's anger but by his own.

"Forgive me, I—" He could say no more.

Rudi's father softened his tone. "Eryk, you have known me for years. And you know that I'm not ashamed to be a Jew any more than I'm ashamed to be a Christian. If our people must suffer, I will suffer with them. The Nazis—"

He had no time to finish. His voice was drowned out by the piercing sound of the air-raid siren.

Mr. Serdusek turned to Salek. "Come—quickly, Salek. We must get to your mother!"

"Wait," shouted Rudi's father. "It's better if the boys stay here; I'll go with you!" Mr. Serdusek scrambled from the trench and out of sight. Rudi's father turned to the boys. "Crouch down as low as you can," he shouted, "and don't get up for any reason!" Then he too leaped from the trench and was gone.

"Look, Rudi, look at the sky," whispered Salek. "There must be hundreds of them." Rudi looked up. The planes seemed very far away, and had it not been for the sound of the siren, he would not have known that there was danger. But suddenly the planes began to swoop down, one after another.

Salek grabbed his arm. "They're coming Rudi! They're coming!"

Moments seemed like hours as they watched the planes draw nearer. Rudi began to feel as if a leaden weight were pressing on his chest. His stomach started knotting up, and his mouth became so dry that he could hardly swallow. Then came the deafening explosions—one after another, and each more terrible than the last. *Oh, Lord, please,*

please don't let them hit us! he prayed. It was as if the whole earth were caving in, and he could do nothing but wait, wait for it to come tumbling down upon him. He wanted desperately to scream, to cry out. But he could not.

All at once, Salek stood upright in the trench. "We've got to run—to get away, Rudi!" Rudi tried to pull him down, but Salek kicked at him and screamed. "We'll be buried alive—I tell you we'll be buried alive!" Rudi pulled with all his strength and at last succeeded in knocking Salek off his feet. Once he had him down, he tried to hold him there. He forgot even his fear. All his strength, all his concentration centered on keeping Salek in the trench.

At last the bombings ceased. Salek quieted and Rudi released his hold upon him. The boys sat side by side in silence for a long time. At length Rudi turned to his friend. Salek's hands still trembled as they rested on his knees.

"I never knew that I could be so scared," said Rudi quietly.

Salek continued staring at the dirt wall before him and only said, "I'm not afraid anymore. Please, don't tell my father."

CHAPTER FOUR
THE FIRST LESSON
SEPT. 1939

And Jesus called a little child unto him, and set him in the midst of them.

—Matthew 18:2

"Quickly, boys," Dr. Kaplan said. "Salek, you will come with me. I must go to the hospital. I can see you home on the way. Your family's safe. The worst part of the bombing was in the central part of the city." He turned to Rudi. "God willing, our apartment building is as we left it. I want you to run home as fast as you can. Get as many blankets as you can carry, and bring them to the hospital. I'll meet you there."

As Rudi turned to go, he looked toward the city, and even from a distance he could see the horrible destruction. It stunned him. "Run, Rudi, run," his father urged him gently.

Rudi obeyed and ran as he had never run before—deeper and deeper into what seemed to be an endless nightmare. He found himself leaping over piles of rubble and darting past dead horses, wrecked carriages, and bewildered people. Faster and faster he ran, trying to blur the images that kept rising up before him. But speed offered little relief, for it did nothing to clear the air of the smoke that burned his eyes and the smell of death that made him gasp with every breath.

He did not—he could not—stop until he reached the street on which he lived. There he breathed more freely, for he saw that houses stood, trolley cars yet lined the streets, and autumn leaves swayed gently in the breeze.

Remembering the urgency in his father's voice, he entered the apartment building and dashed up the stairs. He collected as many blankets as he could hold and retraced his steps through the city.

He rushed through the entrance of the hospital. But once inside, he stopped, for he was completely unprepared for what he saw. Crumbled buildings and dead animals were bad enough, but here lay row upon row of men, women, and children, suffering. He did not know how long he stood before his father came to him.

"Rudi, I need your help," he said.

The words stuck in Rudi's throat. "I—I can't—"

His father knelt beside him. "I wouldn't ask you if there were any other way."

"But papa," he whispered, "I—I'm afraid."

"I know you are, son. Still, you must try to forget yourself and think of these people. We can help them, Rudi."

Rudi could say nothing.

"I will not force you to do what you cannot," his father said at length. "But I must ask you to try—just try, son."

Rudi closed his eyes a moment and tried very hard to think clearly. He knew in his heart that he should not run away. But at the same time, he did not see how he could stay. He stood several moments, feeling the pressure of his father's hand upon his shoulder. Then he opened his eyes and took a deep breath. "I'll try, papa."

"That's all I ask," his father said. "I want you to take the blankets and cover those who have no covering. I'll be back to help you in a few minutes." Rudi began moving toward the hallway.

"Rudi." Rudi turned and found his father was once again beside him. "Remember, son," he said, "you're most afraid when you can think of no one but yourself."

As Rudi slowly began his journey down the hall, he tried frantically to think of a way to cover the wounded without looking on them. But he could think of nothing, and sooner than he wished, he found himself standing over a young soldier whose shirt was drenched with blood. He set down all but one of the blankets. Then, trying to appear calm, he started to unfold the one. But in spite of his efforts, he knew that every movement showed his desperation.

At last he succeeded in drawing the blanket up over the young man's shoulders. As he did, he looked into his face. The soldier tried to speak, but could not. Yet Rudi understood that he was grateful. And as he continued his task, he found that it was easier if he looked into the faces of the sufferers, for he saw again and again in their expressions that same touch of gratitude. And such gratitude gave him the courage to go on.

But at the end of the hall, when he came upon a little girl no more than four, again his courage failed him. He hesitated a few feet from her. Unlike the others, Rudi noticed that she did not suffer from wounds received in the air raid's violent explosions. Instead, she had been shot in her right shoulder and forearm. And though she must have been in pain, she was not crying as the other children. She lay very still, very quiet, her pale face looking almost transparent against the dark wooden floor. Rudi could see that she needed covering, but he felt for some reason that to disturb her now would only increase her

suffering. Before he could decide what he should do, his father came to him. Motioning for Rudi to join him, he started toward the little girl. But Rudi caught him by the arm.

"Papa," he said quietly, "how was she hurt?"

"From what I understand, she was with her sister, digging for potatoes in a field outside the city. Since the air-raid sirens had ceased, I imagine they thought they'd be safe. But a German fighter plane returned, dived down, and riddled the field with machine-gun fire."

"Where's her sister?" asked Rudi. His father shook his head. Rudi understood.

"How old was she?"

"About your age," said Rudi's father.

"Where are the parents?"

"I've not been able to locate them."

"Has she told you what her name is?"

"She has not made a sound since one of the soldiers brought her here."

"Surely she can talk," Rudi said.

"Maybe there's nothing that she cares to say."

Together they moved toward the little girl. When she saw them approaching, she turned away from them and shuddered. And by the time they knelt beside her, her breathing had become so rapid that she could scarcely catch her breath.

Rudi covered her with blankets while his father softly brushed the hair out of her eyes. Dr. Kaplan continued resting his hand on her forehead until she breathed more easily. He then gave her an injection and sat down to wait for the shot to take effect before bandaging her wounds.

After a few moments she again lay very still. At length, she turned and looked at Rudi. As she did, he noticed that her eyes began to fill with tears, and though she remained silent, he felt that now it was right for him to sit beside her.

His father sensed the change as well and seemed to search for words. Finding none, he reached into his shirt pocket, pulled out a small testament, opened it, and began to read. "And Jesus came and touched them and said, . . . be not afraid." His voice was as deep as the rumbling of thunder, but as gentle as a summer rain. And Rudi thought, as he listened to his father and watched the little girl, how glad he was that he had been there to sit beside her—how glad he was that he had not run away.

CHAPTER FIVE
THE FALL
SEPT. 1939

The show of their countenance doth witness against them.
—Isaiah 3:9a

Rudi did not forget the lessons he had learned that first day. There was no time for forgetting, because the air raids not only continued but increased, and for the next two weeks he and his father spent every waking moment at the hospital.

"Here, this will help," said Rudi as he offered an old man some water.

"I don't want any," the old man said.

"You must, sir. It'll help, honest."

"I don't want it, I tell you," he replied gruffly.

"The boy's just trying to help," said a young soldier in the next bed.

"I don't want help! We're lost. You and I know it, and he might as well know it too. Have you been outside, boy?" he asked, turning to Rudi. "What do you see? I'll tell you. You see ashes—that's all that's left—ashes." He turned his face to the wall.

Rudi stood staring at the old man until the young soldier spoke again. "I'll take some of that water."

Rudi left the old man and moved to the young soldier's bed.

"Don't mind him," the young man said quietly as he took a cup from Rudi. "He's been at the front. Not much food and a lot of strain out there. His nerves are shattered. His home's gone too, and he can't find his family. He just needed to let off steam, and you happened to be standing there."

"I'm sorry," said Rudi.

The soldier smiled. "No need for you to be sorry. Now if the Germans want to offer us an apology—that's different!"

"Do you think there's any hope?" asked Rudi.

The soldier's smile faded. "I suppose that depends on what you mean by hope," he said. "It looks as if the Germans may get the upper hand for a while—I can't deny that. But we'll come out all right in the end. The Poles are a tough lot."

Rudi hesitated. "But—what about the Jews? Do you think they'll come out all right?"

"If they're Polish Jews," the soldier said, "they'll come out all right." He handed Rudi his empty cup, and his smile returned just as Dr. Kaplan entered the ward.

"Poland has fallen," Rudi's father said.

The old man kept his face to the wall, and the young soldier ceased smiling and stared at nothing. The silence grew so heavy that Rudi felt as if he could reach out and touch it, and he was grateful when his father finally spoke again.

"The only comfort I can offer you," he said, "is the comfort that I have in my own heart. That is this: we are not in the hands of the Germans, but in the hands of God."

Rudi followed his father out into the hall, where they found Salek and Mr. Serdusek waiting.

"More news?" asked Rudi's father, greeting them.

"Just details, none of which you'll like hearing," said Mr. Serdusek.

"But ones we must listen to anyway, I take it."

"Yes," continued Mr. Serdusek. "But first, before I forget—here." He reached into his pocket and pulled out two small cards. "Ration cards from the Jewish Council."

Rudi's father hesitated.

"Take them, Jakob," Salek's father urged. "You are a Jew, aren't you?"

"Thank you, Eryk," said Rudi's father as he took the cards.

"You'll need them from now on. The food situation isn't going to get any better, and the Germans certainly won't help us. They'll pass out bread to the Gentiles for propaganda purposes, but even that won't last long. So, we at the Council are trying to provide Jews with at least enough to stay alive. It won't be much more than bread and soup, but it's something."

"There are still a few butcher's shops left," said Rudi. "We can get some meat there and maybe stock up for the—"

Salek interrupted him. "Forget it. They've closed."

"They saw what was coming," Mr. Serdusek explained. "If there were any left standing, they closed their doors by noon. So did the remaining bakeries. I think most of them plan to keep the extra food for their own families. I can't blame them for that. Anyway, it's going to get much worse before it gets better."

"We'll manage," said Rudi's father.

Rudi was not so sure. He could not imagine a day without sweet rolls for breakfast and meat for supper. Soup was all right for lunch—sometimes.

"I don't know how you've managed to house and feed so many these past few days," Dr. Kaplan said.

"The same way you have managed to keep so many alive," Mr. Serdusek told him. "We do what we must."

"Do you think the Germans will allow the Council to continue aiding Jews?" asked Dr. Kaplan.

Mr. Serdusek paused, and his typical air of self-confidence dissolved. Rudi had never seen him look so unsure.

"I don't know," he said. "I only know that they are aware of our work. Already they have sent a messenger to the Council, instructing us to hand over our list of the Jewish residents in Warsaw."

Rudi's father looked shocked. "You're giving them such a list?"

"We've not yet decided what to do," Mr. Serdusek replied, "but we may have to."

"They'll treat us better if we do," Salek interjected.

"We hope," Mr. Serdusek cautioned. "It seems, from what has gone on in other cities, that they are less severe with the Jews who cooperate. It may be best not to antagonize them. Still—I will not give them such a list until first I know their mind."

"Don't we already know what the Germans think of Jews?" asked Rudi.

"There are those reports from Berlin and Lodz," added Dr. Kaplan.

"Surely those reports are somewhat exaggerated," said Mr. Serdusek, but his tone seemed to contradict his words. "Perhaps once we understand the German mind, we can reason with them." Rudi watched the old air of confidence return as he added, "As a lawyer I have spent my life studying the minds of my opponents. That is how I win. I will win this battle the same way."

"I hope you can," said Rudi's father. "Believe me, I hope you can."

"Now to matters at hand," Mr. Serdusek continued. "The Germans will enter the city this evening. They have sent some of their officers ahead, instructing us to 'clean' the main streets for them. I'm going now to round up some volunteers."

"You must be joking!" said Dr. Kaplan.

"I wish I were."

"But the bombs—the whole city's wrecked!" exclaimed Rudi.

"They know that," said Mr. Serdusek bitterly. "Still, they want us to 'tidy up' so they can walk through the central part of town in a military fashion. Hitler's men must do things in military fashion!"

"It's impossible," said Dr. Kaplan.

Mr. Serdusek turned to go, saying, "Well, you must admit, it's not the first time we've been called upon to do the impossible. Oh, yes, there is one more thing," he added. "All of us are expected to line the streets as they march in. They not only expect clean streets but a welcoming committee. We must greet them with due 'pomp and ceremony.' "

"I don't want to greet any Nazis," Salek protested.

"You will greet them with the rest of us," his father said.

"But you hate the Germans," argued Salek.

"Yes, but I will do what I must to survive," said his father. "And so will you." Then turning back to Dr. Kaplan, he asked, "You will come?"

"I haven't time."

"Jakob, they will be watching."

"I can't leave here."

Mr. Serdusek hesitated a moment and then said, "Maybe it will be obvious—even to a German—why you cannot be there. But you must make Rudi go."

Dr. Kaplan paused. "All right," he said, giving in. "If you'll take care of him."

"I'll bring him back here myself when it's over. Rudi, meet us at the corner of our street at 6:00."

"Did you hear that we must all turn in our radios?" asked Salek, who had run ahead of his father to meet Rudi.

"Our radios? Who said?" asked Rudi.

"Papa. The Germans sent more orders to the Jewish Council members. I was with him when they came. You should see the list."

"Why in the world do they want our radios?" said Rudi. "That's stupid!"

Salek shrugged. "Maybe they're afraid we'll find out that the English and French are beating them."

"I hope they are—crazy Nazis," Rudi muttered just as Mr. Serdusek came up to join them.

They continued on in silence until they reached the center of town. There they took their places among the conquered, and as the distant pounding of marching feet drew nearer, Rudi's imagination grew more active. What would Hitler's soldiers look like?

At last the regiments reached the place where Rudi stood. He looked carefully at the black-booted men in smart-looking uniforms. Despite the pomp, some of them looked very ordinary. Others, however, did not. As he stared into these "other" faces, his mind went back to the story of the trumpeter. Indeed, these were the faces of "a fierce, unfeeling people"—a people that would not hesitate to shoot children in the fields.

As they passed out of sight, he looked out over the city. It was the first time since the bombings started that he had allowed himself a moment to stand quietly and take in what had happened. Most of the museums, libraries, and palaces were all gone—so was his favorite cathedral. A deep uneasiness came over him, for he realized that nothing was—nor ever could be—as it once had been.

CHAPTER SIX
JEWS OUT!
OCT. 1939

Our inheritance is turned to strangers, our houses to aliens.

—Lamentations 5:2

"No—no! Please!"

Rudi opened his eyes. He thought he was having another nightmare until he heard the second cry. "Let me go with them—please take me with them!" Rudi recognized the voice. It was Mrs. Kaminsky. She and her family lived on the first floor of the apartment building.

"We have come only for Jews!" a German soldier shouted.

Rudi sat up and saw his father standing at his window, looking down at the street below.

"Rudi, get up quickly," he said. "Put on two pair of trousers, two shirts, two sweaters, and your coat as well." He then turned from the window, went to the wardrobe that stood in the corner of Rudi's room, and pulled out a few small articles of clothing. He tucked the clothing down inside his shirt, then headed for the door. "Come into the front room as soon as you are dressed—and hurry," he said.

37

Rudi could yet hear the Kaminsky children crying in the street. He wanted to run to the window and look out, but he knew there was no time. He moved as fast as he could. Still, it had never taken him so long to dress. His arms and legs seemed unwilling to cooperate.

"Don't hurt the children!" he heard Mr. Kaminsky shouting. "Give me time—I'll lift them up into the truck once I get inside!"

Suddenly someone started the vehicle. The motor drowned out the sound of voices—but not for long. Once the truck pulled away, Rudi again heard Mrs. Kaminsky's pleading. "Wait! Please—let me go with them." Her cry was so desperate, so full of anguish that he was overwhelmed by a feeling of helplessness, and for a moment he stopped what he was doing.

Then another truck pulled up and the sound of the heavy boots of soldiers on the stairs forced him once again to action. He could now hear the soldiers on the third floor, beating their nightsticks against the wooden doors. Then he heard them shouting. "Jews out! No! Leave everything—including the keys. Put them in the keyhole!"

He finished dressing and rushed into the front room. His father was taking some things out of his desk and concealing them inside his heavy coat. He then took the small Bible that was lying on the table and dropped it inside Rudi's jacket pocket. By this time, the soldiers had reached the fourth floor and were in the next apartment. "Come here and stand beside me," his father said. "Say nothing. We shall do as they say."

The pounding started. Rudi moved closer to his father just as a soldier burst through the door. Before the German even spoke, Dr. Kaplan handed him the keys and moved toward the stairs. He kept Rudi directly in front of him. The soldier followed close behind. When they reached the first floor landing, Rudi saw that the second truck had disappeared. The soldier gave no instructions. He simply shouted, "Jews out!" Then he shoved his nightstick into Dr. Kaplan's back and thrust them out into the street.

Dr. Kaplan wasted no time in moving away from the building. But they had gotten only halfway up the street when another truck appeared. "Jews! There!" the soldier yelled to the driver. Quickly Dr. Kaplan turned down a darkened side street. Rudi heard the truck screech to a halt just as his father pulled him into a doorway, and before he realized what was happening, he found himself standing inside a dimly lighted shop.

"Thank you, Elias," he heard his father say. By then he had recognized the small man with the long white beard who stood before him. His name was Elias Paderowski, the owner of an antique shop. Rudi had often passed his shop and looked through the windows, but he had never entered. It was full of beautiful things—things that you loved to look at but feared to touch.

Rudi heard the soldiers once again. They were outside the shop shouting to one another. "This way," Elias said. Dr. Kaplan kept a tight hold on Rudi's hand as they moved through the shop to a back door. "Go through that alcove. There is a gutted shop; cut through there. It will quickly get you to the part of town that is filled with nooks and crannies. The Germans will grow weary looking for you."

Once Rudi and his father had passed through the building, the soldiers' voices began to fade. Still, Dr. Kaplan did not slacken his pace.

"Where are we going?" whispered Rudi.

"I think the safest place will be somewhere where the Germans would not want to set up housekeeping."

"Set up housekeeping?" Rudi stopped. "You mean they threw us out because they are going to live in our apartment?"

"Yes, I believe that's what they're going to do."

Dr. Kaplan continued to weave his way through the darkest parts of the city. By the time they had reached their destination, the sun was coming up. Rudi was not encouraged by what he saw, for they had come to the poorest part of Warsaw. Before he could protest, however, his father spied a gutted building and motioned for Rudi to follow him.

At first it was hard to tell what kind of building it had been. But as they moved through the debris, they found machines and remnants of furniture that convinced them that it had been an old office building. At length they came to one office that seemed better than the rest. Though its door swung loosely on the hinges and the windows were no more than bits and pieces of jagged glass, the walls were still intact.

"I think this will do," said Dr. Kaplan as he stepped into the room.

Rudi was shocked. "You mean to live in?"

"Of course to live in," said his father. "And I'll have you know that it took me a long time to find a place that suited me," he added.

"I don't think I like your taste, papa," Rudi told him.

"No? Why it's even furnished," he said cheerfully. "Look, here's a bed."

"That's not a bed. That's a sofa with a big hole in the middle."

"What did I tell you—a bed!"

"O.K. It's a bed," said Rudi. "As long as you're the one that sleeps in the hole."

"I wouldn't have it any other way. I like a sense of adventure—that's why I chose this place, and I still can't see why you don't find it fascinating. Why, look here. We even have pictures." Dr. Kaplan picked up a painting whose canvas hung limply from a two-sided frame.

Rudi took the picture from him to examine it. "Be careful," his father warned. "Your hospital pay wouldn't cover it if you damaged such a masterpiece."

"Speaking of my pay . . ." Rudi began.

"Yes—well—back to paintings."

For several minutes Rudi watched his father dash about the room pointing out their new-found "treasures." He looked something like a fussy old museum guard describing an exhibit to a tour. By the time he finished, Rudi was laughing harder than he had laughed in weeks.

"Papa," said Rudi, becoming serious once again, "do you think we will be able to go back home—just once—to get some things we want? I don't mean anything big. Just—well, you know, personal things."

"I'm afraid not, son. Why do you think I made you put on all those clothes? Why do you think I carried all these things buttoned up in my coat? No, they will not allow us to go back. Nor would they have allowed us to take out what we did had they noticed."

"We can't let them do that, papa!"

"What are we to do, son? Go back and fight them? Go back and face their guns and sticks with our bare hands and throw them out? No. That is not the answer."

"But what will they do with all our things?" Rudi asked.

"I suppose they will steal what they want and leave the rest. But I don't want you to dwell on that. I want you to think how fortunate we are that we were not carried away to work camps as others—like Mr. Kaminsky and his children."

"Papa, why didn't they take Mrs. Kaminsky when they took her family?" Rudi asked more quietly.

"She is a Gentile," he said, and for several moments he seemed lost in other thoughts. Soon, however, he turned back to Rudi and took him by the hand. "The Lord has allowed us to have each other," he said. "That is more than enough."

Though Rudi had to admit that he was glad he had his father, he was not willing to accept that it was enough.

Dr. Kaplan tried once again to sound cheerful. "I think I need to put some finishing touches on our new home before heading to the hospital."

"I'll help," Rudi said reluctantly.

"No, no," his father said. "You and I don't have the same taste, remember? Besides, I think you've earned a bit of time off. Why don't you run over and see Salek. Let the Serduseks know where we live. You might also ask Mrs. Serdusek if she has a few extra dishes and blankets we could use. They should be up by now."

"What if they were kicked out of their house too?" asked Rudi.

"I doubt they were," his father replied. "Their neighborhood is completely Jewish. Most Nazis would rather live in the street than in a Jewish neighborhood."

"Well, they sure don't mind living in our apartment, and we're Jews!"

"We lived in a Gentile section of town. The only Jews there were Christians like us or Jews who were married to Gentiles, like Mr. Kaminsky. According to Hitler's standards, throwing us out was like 'cleaning up' the neighborhood."

"That's ridiculous!" said Rudi.

"Of course it is," his father told him. "It is always ridiculous to imagine yourself superior to other people. Still, lots of people do."

"Hitler's not like most people—he's a lot worse," Rudi said.

"There's where you are wrong. The only difference between his pride and the pride of a common boaster is one of degree."

"What do you mean?" asked Rudi.

"Well, I'm sure you've heard someone brag before, and I'm also sure you've watched others laugh at such a person behind his back. Bragging tends to make the boaster look ridiculous," his father said. "The problem is that pride seldom stops at boasting. A boy may begin by talking about how smart he is. But eventually you find that he doesn't just brag on himself; he begins to criticize those who may do as well as or better than he does. Eventually, he is not satisfied to stop at criticizing such people, for he feels that they threaten him. So he sets out to destroy them. Pride is a frightening vice, though it may not look so in its early stages. But a man who lets pride get hold of him will soon cease behaving like a simple fool and start acting like a devil."

"Like Hitler," said Rudi.

"Exactly. I'd say that the *Führer* is very far along in the school of pride."

"What about all those people who believe in him?" asked Rudi. "Are they just fools?"

"You mean like the soldiers who threw us out tonight?"

"Yes, and all the rest of the Germans."

"Well, I doubt that all the Germans believe him. Many know him for the evil man he is and are probably just afraid or unable to oppose him. For most of those who do follow him, I would say, yes, they are still just fools. He has given them food and work and appealed to their vanity, telling them that they are a superior race of men and women. If they continue to follow him, however, they will become as evil as he is. It's a valuable lesson for us. Though a good man may compliment you, he will also— in love—acknowledge your weaknesses. But you should never trust a man who tries to win your favor solely by appealing to your pride."

"I doubt I'll have to worry about that anytime soon."

"Probably not," his father laughed. "But seriously, son, I would rather be in our position than theirs."

"I'm not so sure I can say that, papa," said Rudi.

"Then try to stand back from the situation a bit and look at it the way God does. He sees what they are doing to His people, Rudi, and He won't ignore it."

"That doesn't seem to do much good now," said Rudi.

"I wouldn't say that, son—especially in your case and mine. We may not have all the comforts we're used to, but we still know that Christ loves us and will care for us. He proved that tonight by protecting us. We can continue to rest in God's mercy. But those who trust in Hitler have nothing to look forward to but God's wrath."

CHAPTER SEVEN
A SECRET PLAN
OCT. 1939

*So I returned, and considered all the oppressions that
are done under the sun: and behold the tears of such
as were oppressed, and they had no comforter; and on
the side of their oppressors there was power; but they
had no comforter.*

—Ecclesiastes 4:1

As Rudi set out for Salek's, his mind was filled with
the events of the early morning. He heard again Mrs.
Kaminsky's pleading, the children's weeping, and the
soldiers' shouting. Then he imagined once more the soldier
who had broken through their door. How clearly he
recalled this German's face. It reminded him of white
stone—smooth and hard. He could not imagine that such
a man had ever laughed except in scorn. Then came the
worst thought of all—the thought that this soldier might
at that very moment be standing in his room. Could that
really be possible? The thought so gripped him that he
stopped, turned, and headed toward his old neighborhood.

He was surprised how easy it was for him to remember
the maze of twisted streets and alleys he and his father
had taken only hours before. The daylight, however,

exposed the wretchedness of the path that the darkness had concealed, and he decided to be brave and venture out into a more open, familiar route.

He was almost home when he heard the sound of breaking glass. It stopped, then started, stopped and started again. He continued on, but stayed closer to the buildings. When he turned the last corner, he saw Elias Paderowski standing just outside his shop. A soldier stood beside him, and all about them were mounds of broken glass. Rudi froze, for just then a second soldier came out of the shop holding a beautiful vase above his head. The soldier hesitated only long enough to glance into Elias's face, and then he smashed the vase on the street before him. He then reentered the shop and returned with another antique. Again he broke the priceless treasure at the old man's feet. Elias said nothing, but Rudi could see that tears were streaming down his weathered face and disappearing into his full, white beard.

"See what happens to Aryans who help Jews!" Rudi turned to see a Gestapo officer standing over him. The German grabbed him and turned him around once more to face the scene. "Look! Look!" he said, his iron grip digging into Rudi's shoulder. "Such sights will teach you never to make the same mistake!" The officer then released his hold and said, "You are free to go. Just don't forget what you have learned."

At first Rudi was too confused to grasp what the man had said, and he did not move. "Go, you stupid Polish boy!" the officer shouted.

Then it hit him—this German had no idea that Rudi was a Jew. Quickly he turned and left. But as he did, anger welled up inside of him—an anger so strong that it pushed aside every fear and hardened his determination into granite. The thought that such men could sleep in his bed, ransack his room, and rummage through those

things that he had saved and treasured for years filled him with rage. It was too dangerous for him to go home now, but as he headed toward Salek's, he promised himself, *I will go back! I will!*

"Are you crazy!" Salek shouted.

"I have to go back," said Rudi.

"Do you know what'll happen to you if they catch you in there?"

"It's my house," Rudi said bitterly.

"Not anymore," Salek told him. "What do you plan to do anyway? Walk in with a cart and haul out your stuff right under their nose?"

"I only want one thing," said Rudi.

"What—what can be that important?"

Rudi hesitated then said, "I'll tell you if I get it."

"If you're alive to tell me anything. Rudi, listen to me. Papa's told me of the things they're doing to people who try to get back into their houses. If you're caught—and I don't see how you can avoid it—they'll shoot you, right then. They don't care whose house it is. To them we're all just Jews, and Jews are—"

"I know what they think," Rudi said irritably. "And I know what they'll do to me if I get caught. But I don't intend to get caught. The soldiers can't stay in the apartments all day long."

"Rudi, we can't even walk through the neighborhood. It's 'Aryan,' remember."

"Nobody will know I'm Jewish," he protested, remembering his recent encounter with the German soldier. "I don't look like a Jew."

Salek shook his head in disbelief. "And you don't think they'll figure it out when you go walking up the stairs to your apartment?"

"I don't plan to go in the front door," he replied. "They won't even know I've been there. I'll get in through the alley somehow."

"Rudi, you're four stories up—you got wings or something?"

"Don't be an idiot," said Rudi. "You've been mountain climbing before; you can show me how to get in."

"We're not talking about mountains—"

"Mountains, buildings, what's the difference?" argued Rudi.

Salek shook his head.

"Look, Salek, all I want you to do is help me plan it," Rudi pleaded. "Can't you just help me do that much?"

"Rudi," said Salek. "Can't you understand how rotten I'd feel if something happened to you—especially if I helped you plan it all? This lousy war is bad enough."

"That's one reason I want you to help me—I don't want anything to happen, and two heads are always better than one. Come on, Salek. I can't explain to you how important this is to me—I don't even know if I can explain it to myself—all I know is that I have to try. And, Salek, you're the only one I can trust with this."

"Maybe if you talked to your father—"

"No, this is one time I don't think papa understands. Besides, I know you're good at rescue plans. We've been planning them for years."

"All right," said Salek quietly. "But this one's for real, Rudi. Just don't forget that."

"I won't," Rudi said earnestly. "I promise we'll plan it all out carefully. And I'll practice—practice until I have it all down just right. We can start right now if you like."

"We'd better," Salek told him. "I have a feeling we're gonna need all the time we can get."

"Great!" said Rudi.

"Now listen to me," said Salek. "The first thing we need to do is figure out a back-street route into your old neighborhood. I don't care what you say about not looking Jewish; it's stupid to risk being questioned."

"I've got that figured out already," Rudi told him. "I can use the same route papa and I used when they kicked us out."

"Do you remember all the streets?" asked Salek.

"Yes—" Rudi started to tell him of his trip that morning but stopped, deciding that he wanted to waste no time talking about the past. "Here, I'll draw the map and show you exactly how it works."

Once the map was drawn, they began to figure out how Rudi would get into the apartment.

"There always seem to be soldiers patrolling the main streets," said Rudi.

"How do you plan to get by them?" Salek asked.

"If I take this route, I can get into the alley without having to pass any."

"Now for the hard part—four stories up," Salek added.

"Don't you have something that I could use to climb up to the window? It has a sort of railing and bars around it, like a small terrace."

Salek left the room and returned moments later, carrying a long rope attached to a grappling iron. "We'll have to tie a rag or something around this iron piece so it doesn't clang," he said. "Which reminds me of another important point. You're going to have to do a lot of practicing. I don't mean a day or two. I mean weeks. You gotta get it just right. You don't have all day to stand in the alley, pitching this thing up to the terrace."

"It shouldn't be all that hard," said Rudi.

"It's harder than it looks," said Salek. "The first time papa and I went climbing, I never did get it right. He said he wouldn't take me again until I'd learned. So when we got home, I practiced—for weeks."

"But you know how now?" Rudi asked hopefully.

"Yeah, I know how. Another thing: once you're inside, don't leave this thing hanging over the railing," Salek warned him. "Someone may pass through the alley while you're inside. If they see this hanging there, there's bound to be trouble."

"You're right," Rudi agreed. "And that reminds me— I should probably make several trips to the apartment, just to spy on them. I need to know their schedule."

"Terrific," said Salek, throwing the rope on his bed. "Now you want to visit the Nazis not just once but several times!"

"Think about it. I'll be a lot safer in the end if I know the hours they keep."

"You're right," said Salek. "And who knows, maybe if they spot us two or three times, they'll mistake us for neighbors instead of Jews."

"Us?" said Rudi.

"Yeah, us. I've decided I'm going with you. You need a lookout while you're inside." he said.

"No, Salek. I don't want you taking any chances."

"Too bad," said Salek, "I'm going anyway. I said the same thing to you, and you're still determined to go." Rudi said nothing. Salek had made his point.

Now that the air raids had ceased, the work at the hospital had leveled off. Dr. Kaplan encouraged Rudi to spend more time with Salek. The suggestion was perfect, for they now had ample time to lay their secret plan.

They spent the first week scouting out Rudi's old neighborhood. They became familiar with every back street, every alcove, every alley. They even investigated the deserted shops and buildings along the route and found that by cutting through such places they could reach their destination in half the time. They changed their map accordingly.

Rudi found that two Germans had moved into his apartment. As far as he could tell, their schedules seemed varied. Both men, however, were gone from 3:00 to 5:00 every afternoon. Rudi felt that two hours would give him plenty of time to make his entrance and escape. Salek was not so sure. Still, they both agreed that it was all the time they were going to get.

Once the schedule was set, Rudi turned his attention to the problem of getting into the apartment. Salek had been right: attaching a grappling iron to a terrace was harder than it looked. But he was determined. He spent hours with Salek outside an old apartment building in the Serduseks' neighborhood. No one seemed to notice their practicing. Rudi figured that the people had seen so many frightful sights the past few weeks that even the most extraordinary activity was now no more than ordinary.

By the middle of the second week, Rudi could attach the iron to a terrace railing with ease. He then set about to master the task of climbing up the rope. Though he must have tried a hundred times that first day, he could not make it up more than halfway.

"Slow down," Salek warned him. "You're going to kill yourself."

By the next morning Rudi began to wish that he had. The muscles in his arms, shoulders, and back were so sore that he could scarcely move. But in spite of the pain, he got up, dressed, and went out to climb again.

Salek had little idea of the powerful emotions that spurred Rudi on. It seemed as soon as he touched the rope, his mind filled with all the images of the past few weeks. One after another they came to him. They drove him, forced him on until his hands grew calloused and his muscles became as taut as the tightly woven rope.

"I can't believe how fast you're learning to do this," Salek said. "You'll be ready in no time."

"I am ready," Rudi told him.

CHAPTER EIGHT
TRAPPED!
NOV. 1939

He that is slow to anger is better than the mighty; and he that ruleth his spirit than he that taketh a city.
—Proverbs 16:32

The next morning when Rudi arrived at Salek's, the early morning frost still lingered on the windows. He pressed his hand against the glass, and the crystals melted beneath his touch. Seeing that Mrs. Serdusek was already in the kitchen and Salek was already underfoot, he knocked.

After breakfast the boys retreated to Salek's room to discuss final preparations for their adventure. One concern was how to carry the equipment. Rudi didn't want to be burdened down; he wanted to be as free as possible for crawling, climbing—or running. After some discussion, they decided that it would be best to detach the grappling iron from the rope. Rudi could take care of the rope by winding it again and again around his waist. Salek could take care of the iron by hooking it to his belt and hiding it under his heavy winter coat. Once they had decided how to handle the equipment, they reviewed their map and entrance plans. By 2:30 that afternoon they were on their way.

Everything was going according to plan until they passed the halfway mark and Rudi suddenly suggested, "Here, Salek, let's cut through this building."

Salek shook his head. "Let's stick to the map."

"Aw, come on," Rudi urged. "I'm sure the place is deserted. Besides, if we do, we'll be skipping a street and buying a bit more time."

"All right." Reluctantly Salek followed Rudi into the building.

Rudi was relieved to find that he had been right—the building was deserted. He soon discovered, however, that his idea was definitely not the way to save time, for as soon as they stepped outside, he saw two guards lounging at the end of the alley—looking right toward them.

"Oh, no!" said Salek in a hoarse whisper.

He had barely gotten the words out before one of the guards yelled, "Hey, you there!"

"Get going!" cried Rudi as he shoved Salek back inside the building.

The shrill sound of police whistles started as he and Salek dashed out into one alley and down another. Rudi gave little heed to their direction. He wanted only to put distance between him and Salek and their pursuers. He was beginning to think he had succeeded—then they rounded the corner. In an instant a young German soldier reached and collared Salek.

Rudi turned on him in a fury, "Let him go! Let him go, I say!"

At that moment someone grabbed him from behind, pulled him back, and shook him. "Stop it! Stop it, boy."

Rudi looked up. His captor was a Pole, a village farmer. The man pushed him—not roughly, but firmly—back against the cart that was blocking the alley. The cart was filled with garbage. Rudi knew that several of the villagers had been forced to use their carts for "cleanup," and he had seen them picking up rubble in the streets and garbage from the relief kitchens. The soldier must have stopped the man to see if he was doing his job well. Rudi calmed down a bit. Even so, the farmer did not release his hold. Instead, he turned toward the young German, "Well?" he said.

The soldier looked at Rudi and then at Salek. The sound of a police whistle started up again. The soldier listened, then studied Salek carefully. "Put them in there," he finally said and pointed toward the cart.

"No!" protested Rudi.

"Shut up, boy," said the farmer sharply. Then he whispered, "Can't you see he's trying to save your hide? Now get in there and bury yourself."

Rudi looked at Salek, and then both of them leaped into the cart and burrowed down beneath the cinders, dirt, and garbage. The cart jerked forward, and the welcome sound of horses' hoofs on the stone street blocked out the noise of their pursuers. They were free—at least for the moment.

They must have traveled about fifteen minutes before the cart came to a stop. "You can get out here," the farmer called back.

"If I were you," the man continued as the boys climbed out, "I'd get home as fast as I could and stay there." With this final admonition, he spurred his horses on.

"Yuk!" Salek exclaimed as soon as the farmer was out of sight.

"That's for sure," Rudi agreed, looking down at himself. "At least we can't hear those whistles anymore," he said. "We're safe now."

"No thanks to you," Salek grumbled as he picked a slimy piece of potato peeling out of his hair. "Where in the world are we anyway?"

"Not where we want to be," Rudi said. "Come on, we need to go this way."

Salek stopped him. "Whoa! Where is 'this way'?"

"To the apartment, of course. Come on, we've wasted enough time."

"That's right," said Salek. "Too much! There's not enough of it left."

"Yes there is—if we hurry. Anyway, do you want to go through this again tomorrow?" asked Rudi.

"You know, Rudi," said Salek, shaking his head, "I really hope the Nazis don't kill you. You know why? 'Cause when we finally get home, I'd like to do it."

The boys crouched behind a coal bin in the alley and looked up at the terrace window. "All right—hand me that iron piece," said Rudi.

Salek reached inside his coat and pulled it out. "I still can't believe that Nazi let us go—especially me," he said, handing over the grappling iron. "I could tell by the way he was staring holes in me that he knew I was a Jew all right."

"I'm sure he had his reasons," Rudi said sullenly, as he continued unwinding the rope from his waist. He was not in the mood to give a German credit for doing anything good. He could think of nothing now but his anger toward them.

"Still," Salek said, "I hope the ones that live up there are like he was."

Rudi made no reply; he was concentrating on securing the iron to the rope.

"Rudi," said Salek, "can you tell me now why you're going in there?"

"Hopefully, you'll know in just a few minutes," said Rudi, and he began to move out.

Salek seemed unwilling to let him go. "Don't you want to take a minute or two more to catch your breath?"

"Like you said, there's no time," Rudi said. And slowly, very slowly, he moved from behind the bin and stood beneath the window.

He twisted one end of the rope loosely around his right hand and let the hooked end dangle from his left. Then taking a deep breath, he began the steady circular motion. *One, two, three,* he counted to himself, then let the iron piece fly into the air. He hit his mark and barely made a sound.

He leaned back and tugged on the rope to be certain it could bear his weight. Then he looked once more at Salek before starting up. When he was almost to the top, he heard a soldier shout in the street. The sound so jarred him that he nearly lost his grip. But he regained himself, and with a sudden burst of energy he pulled himself up and grasped a railing shaft. Then tugging with all his might, he succeeded in swinging his body over the railing and onto the narrow terrace landing. Quickly he pulled the rope up and climbed inside.

He stood again in his father's room and scanned the scene. The Germans had ransacked everything, and had done nothing to conceal their shameful acts. The door of the wardrobe was ajar, and several pieces of his father's clothing lay upon the floor. His father's personal ledgers and notebooks also lay open on his desk, and papers were strewn everywhere.

He crossed to the desk. *They better not have touched my mother's letters,* he said to himself as he dropped the rope in the corner, opened the center desk drawer, and

reached back as far as he could. Relief swept over him as his fingers touched a small leather pouch. The pouch was where his father had placed the two remaining birthday letters Rudi had yet to receive from his mother. He drew the pouch out and opened it—it was empty.

Throwing it aside, he rummaged through the desk drawers, swept the papers from the desk top, and crawled about the floor searching for the letters. He found nothing. A hot rage filled his heart and gave vent to angry tears. He felt as if he must throw or break something. He turned to look for an object that might suit his purpose—then stopped. He heard Salek's warning whistle. But it was too late, for just then he also heard a door key turn inside the lock. He dropped to his knees and slid under the bed.

His heart was pounding wildly and sounded in his ears like the beating of a thousand drums. The door opened, and he heard someone heading toward his father's room. The footsteps stopped just inside the room. From under the bed, Rudi could see the polished black boots of a German soldier. He did not know if the soldier had heard him; he prayed that he had not.

The German moved slowly to the center of the room—*too slowly,* Rudi thought. He then turned and walked over to the desk. Rudi could hear him rustling through the papers. *The rope—O Lord, please don't let him see the rope!* he prayed.

The soldier left the desk and went to the wardrobe. Rudi heard it open and then listened as the soldier rummaged through it. Still, he could not see if the man was putting something away—or looking for something. At length the man closed the wardrobe and came toward the bed. He stopped just at the foot. Rudi could have reached out and touched the German's boot.

Just then the apartment door opened once again. "Franke? You here, Franke?" a husky voice called out.

"In here, Mende," the soldier in the bedroom answered.

Rudi heard the second soldier enter the room. "What do we have to eat?" he demanded.

"You've left us very little, I fear," replied the man named Franke.

"Then I will have to go and convince the grocer to give me more," he heard Mende say. "Would you like to join me? After getting something to eat, I might look around for some entertainment."

"No—I think I'll pass. I'd like to rest."

"Suit yourself," said Mende as he turned to leave. Then as an afterthought he added, "By the way, why in the world do you have the window open?"

Rudi nearly gasped.

"Window?" said Franke. "I don't know, I—" he stopped. "I guess I just forgot about it," he said, and he walked over to the window and shut it.

"You might do well to remember such things— particularly at night," said Mende. "Some of us are not exactly popular in this city." And he laughed.

"Yes, I've noticed that," said Franke quietly.

Mende turned and left the room. Rudi listened and heard the outside door slam. As soon as Mende was gone, Franke seated himself on the bed and began removing his boots. *He must not know that I am here,* thought Rudi, trying to calm himself. But he felt a bit safer once Franke had stretched himself out on the bed.

His feeling of relief, however, did not last long, for it seemed as if suddenly a thousand thoughts rushed into his mind. *How can I escape? I could never make it to the window. And what is Salek doing? Surely he wouldn't risk coming in here after me.*

An uncontrollable fear began to overtake him. He could stand the strain of hiding no longer. He had to get out. He would run; yes, that was it. No—it was impossible.

Once he drew their attention, he knew he could never run fast enough. They would catch him, and then—he must wait. He must control his fear.

As he wrestled with these thoughts, the wintry dusk turned into frigid darkness. For a long time, he lay shivering under the bed, listening to the soldier's breathing. Eventually it settled into a deep, steady rhythm. *It's now or never,* Rudi thought. And he forced himself to stretch his hand out from under the bed and feel the floor. There seemed to be nothing in the way.

God, help me, he prayed as cautiously, very cautiously he began to slide out from his hiding place. At last he lay beside the bed, taking comfort in the darkness that covered him. He could not even see his hand before his face, so he was sure that no one else could see anything, either.

Carefully, he rose to a crawling position. Then feeling the way before him, he proceeded to the door. He continued crawling even when he reached the outer room, for he dared not stand upright. He dared not tempt himself to break into a run. Not until he touched the door did he stand up.

Gently he turned the latch and stepped out into the dimly lighted hall, softly closing the door behind him. He moved to the stairs and stood a few moments clinging to the railing. All the tension had drained out of him, and he felt as if he might faint. It was then he heard a creaking on the stairs. It stopped. *It's just my imagination,* he thought. But then it came again. Someone was definitely coming, and he was trying not to be heard.

He moved back into a corner and pressed himself against the wall. The stranger was coming up the last flight of stairs. As he reached the landing and turned, Rudi saw his face. It was his father.

Rudi's father said nothing all the way home. But as soon as they had reached their room and closed the door behind them, he turned on Rudi. "What in the world were you thinking!"

"Papa, I had to go back—"

"No, Rudi," his father cut him off. "You did not have to go back."

"They took our things!" cried Rudi.

"That apparently is not all they took from you," his father said. "They took your good sense away as well. And if Salek had not come to me, who knows what would have happened!"

"Papa, you don't understand," Rudi protested.

"I understand that you are angry. I'm angry too, Rudi. But that does not justify your risking not only your own life but the life of your best friend as well to go back there!"

"I didn't ask Salek to go. He wanted to go."

"He did it out of love for you, which ought to make you all the more ashamed! Rudi, there is no excuse for what you have done."

"Papa, you don't understand."

"I understand—as you should—the value of human life. People, people are important, Rudi—not things."

"But it wasn't just things. I went back for mama's letters. It's her, papa, those letters were all I had, and I—oh, nobody understands—not even you."

"Rudi." His father walked over and reached inside his doctor's bag. "I would think, knowing me as you do, that you could have trusted me a little more," he said, and he pulled a packet of letters from the bag. "I understand, son. I had them all along."

CHAPTER NINE
THE REIGN OF TERROR
NOV. 1939

We are . . . persecuted, but not forsaken.
—II Corinthians 4:8b-9a

"I think it best for you to join me at the hospital again," said Rudi's father the next morning. "There you can occupy your mind with work rather than with how you have been wronged."

His father's decision did not disappoint Rudi, for he realized that he'd begun to miss the people there and the work.

"First, however," his father continued, "there is something else I want you to do. When you've finished breakfast, I want you to go to the Serduseks' and apologize to Salek and his parents for what happened."

"Yes, papa," said Rudi.

"I'll see you at the hospital as soon as you're done," his father said. Then he put on his coat and left.

Rudi sat in the kitchen alone, thinking about his visit to the Serduseks'. He did not want to go. Though he was not quite ready to admit it, he was beginning to understand how foolish he had been. And he was ashamed. He knew, however, that the longer he put it off, the worse it would be. So, reluctantly, he pushed aside his bread and set out.

Mrs. Serdusek answered the door. As Rudi looked up at her, his shame overwhelmed him, and at that moment nothing in the world seemed as important as forgiveness. "I'm sorry, Mrs. Serdusek," he blurted out. "I'm sorry. I didn't want to hurt Salek, honest. I—"

"Come in, Rudi," she said quietly as she placed her hand on his shoulder. At that moment Salek appeared at the door.

"Rudi! Boy am I glad to see you! I thought—"

Mrs. Serdusek stopped him and led them both into the kitchen. Mr. Serdusek had already gone. As the three of them sat down at the table, Rudi noticed that Salek's mother did not seem like her usual self. She was usually so careful in her dress, and her manner was always kind and cheerful. But today wisps of hair fell carelessly about her drawn face, and her eyes looked dark and troubled.

"Boys," she began, "I don't know if you can understand what I'm going to say, but—well, you must. For if you do, you will never again place yourself in unnecessary danger. You must understand that these men, these Nazis, are unlike anyone you've ever known. They are liars, and they are cruel. Do you know what some of them have told people? They say not only that we are inferior; they say that we sacrifice Christian children for our Passover feasts."

"Nobody could be stupid enough to believe that," Rudi said.

"I used to think that too, Rudi, but now I am not so sure. I am sure, however, that there are Nazis who would murder every Jew if they could. And who knows, there may come a time when—" Mrs. Serdusek stopped.

Salek put his arm around her. "Don't worry, mama. You know that papa says he can learn to reason with them. He will figure out a way to keep us safe."

"Perhaps," she said, trying to force a smile. "Perhaps."

"Besides," Salek continued, "you don't have to worry about me and Rudi. We won't ever do anything as stupid as we did yesterday."

"He's right, Mrs. Serdusek. Honest," said Rudi quickly.

By the time Rudi left Salek's, his conscience was clear, but his mind was somewhat troubled. He could not forget Mrs. Serdusek's worried expression. It was as if she understood something others could not grasp—something frightening.

When Rudi arrived at the hospital, he was still lost in thought. He did not notice the two German officers that stood in the hallway until one of them addressed him.

"You. What is your name?" the soldier said.

Rudi jumped, for he recognized the voice. It was Mende. Rudi's first thought was that Mende had found the rope that he had left behind and had somehow traced it back to him.

"I asked you a question!" Mende snapped.

"Rudi—my name is—is Rudi."

"Rudi what!"

"Kaplan," he replied.

"Kaplan," repeated Mende, and an ugly smile spread across his fleshy face. "Where is your father?"

Rudi did not answer. "You're very poor at answering questions," Mende said as he took his pistol out. He jerked Rudi toward him and placed the gun next to Rudi's temple. But the other officer raised his hand, and reluctantly Mende lowered the gun. It was evident by his uniform that this second officer was of higher rank than Mende.

"We have a message for him," the second soldier said, and Rudi recognized his voice as well. It was Franke.

"Could you go to him and tell him that? We have a message—that is all."

Rudi, glad to be released, ran to find his father. "Papa," he said, "there are officers—they say they have a message for you."

Rudi followed his father back out into the hall. "I am Jakob Kaplan. What is it you want?"

"I am Captain Franke," the officer said calmly. "We have come to tell you that your services are no longer needed."

"You can't be serious," said Dr. Kaplan. "Although things are better than they were—still, every room is filled."

"There are other doctors here," Captain Franke continued. "And—"

"Oh, yes—three others," Rudi's father interrupted. "Three—three for the entire hospital."

"I thought you told me there were six doctors here, Mende," said Franke, turning to his colleague.

"There were," explained Dr. Kaplan, "but three of them have come down with typhoid."

"That doesn't matter," said Mende. "Your services are not needed."

"Not needed? How can you in good conscience stand there and say such a thing?" Rudi's father demanded.

"We do not need a Jew to care for Gentiles!" Mende answered.

"The point is not whether I am a Jew; the point is that I am a doctor, and these people need a doctor."

"We will see that the patients are cared for," Captain Franke replied.

"How? Can you cleanse wounds? Can you remove bullets from flesh? Or perhaps you are better at diagnosing typhoid victims or caring for those who are dying from malnutrition!" continued Dr. Kaplan, growing angry. "Tell me, where, where will you get these doctors? You know that there are not that many left. Those of my colleagues who have not taken ill have been sent off to work camps."

"Enough!" Mende shouted. He again drew his gun.

Rudi's father turned to him and was about to speak when Mende lifted his gun and brought the butt of the pistol down across Rudi's face. As Rudi stumbled beneath the blow, he heard Mende scream, "There—now your services are needed! Jews will care for Jews!" He felt his father's powerful arms about him; then everything went black.

CHAPTER TEN
THE HUMILIATION
NOV. 1939

Reproach hath broken my heart; and I am full of heaviness: and I looked for some to take pity, but there was none; and for comforters, but I found none.
—Psalm 69:20

When they reached their room, Rudi's head was throbbing. His father made him lie down and covered him with his coat and a blanket. For once Rudi was glad for a chance to close his eyes and shut out the light.

When he awoke the next morning, he was in a gloomy mood.

"How are you feeling?" his father asked as he sat down beside him and examined his face.

"I'm all right," Rudi said, though he was not at all sure that he was.

"I thought that today of all days you'd be a little more cheerful," his father told him.

Rudi gave him a puzzled look.

"You don't know what I'm talking about?"

Rudi shook his head.

His father looked as if he might explain himself, but he changed his mind and simply said, "Maybe you will remember later." Then growing serious, he asked, "Are you dizzy?"

"No, not really," said Rudi as he tried carefully sitting up. "What are we going to do now that we can't go back to the hospital?" he asked.

"The one thing we know we can do—care for Jews," his father said, and he reached in his shirt pocket and pulled out a scrap of paper. "I've made a list of all those I know of who need care. Mr. Serdusek can give me the names of many others, I'm sure. Maybe this will turn out for the better." Then he added, "I think there are a couple more rooms in this 'palace' of ours that we can clean up and use. We can start our own clinic. How does that sound?"

"Well, at least we won't have far to walk to get to work," said Rudi.

"That's the spirit," his father told him. "I think I'll go out and notify these on the list. Then I'll stop by the Jewish Council Office to see Mr. Serdusek."

"Let me help," Rudi said.

"No, I'd rather you rest a bit more."

"I've been resting all night," he protested. "I'm all right."

His father still hesitated.

"Besides," Rudi added, "I'd rather be doing something other than just sitting around here shivering. I could get Salek to go with me, and we could notify the people on the list. That way you can go ahead and get the list from the Council Office. Everybody could be notified of our new clinic by this afternoon."

"You're pretty convincing." His father glanced over the list once more. "All right. I think you boys can handle it. Everyone on the list is confined to the Jewish part of town. You shouldn't have any trouble. Just don't go into any of the non-Jewish sectors. Is that clear?"

"Don't worry, papa," Rudi said. "I'm not in the mood to scale any buildings today."

"Well, that's a relief." His father smiled wryly at him. "Then I can expect to see you back here in an hour or so."

Being outside did not lighten Rudi's mood as he had hoped, for as he walked, his mind went back to those times before the war when he used to go to Salek's. There had always been customers going in and out of the shops he passed, and each front window had something interesting to look at. He remembered one glass shop where delicate crystal goblets caught the light and threw back their rainbow of colors to the sun. There had also been a clock shop that always had at least ten to fifteen clocks in the window—all ticking the same rhythm. And there had been a bakery. Rudi's mouth began to water as he remembered the smell of hot sweet rolls. How long had it been since he had eaten anything sweet? Bread—bread and watery soup—that had been it for over a month now, and it looked like that was how things were going to continue.

He began to hurry past the deserted shops with their broken windows, until one particular shop caught his eye. It was one of the few that were still open, and an official-looking document had been posted on the inside of the front window. He stopped to read what it said.

NOVEMBER 10, 1939

Following are a list of people to be shot if any Jew in this neighborhood commits any act of belligerence or aggression.

There must have been over a hundred names on the list. And as Rudi scanned it, he realized that many of them were names he recognized. Some were teachers from his school. Others were doctors and lawyers who were his father's friends. There were clergymen and shopkeepers that he knew as well. The one thing that they all had in common was that they were well known in the city. He read on.

1. If there is any destruction of German property, no matter how small, six people will be shot.

2. If there is any act of violence against a German soldier, no matter how small, eight people will be shot.

3. For the death of any German soldier or civilian, no matter what the cause, twelve or more people will be shot.

On November 9, a rock was thrown which broke the windshield of a German vehicle. As a result, the first six people have been shot.

Of those first six Rudi had heard of only one man; the others he did not know. The thought then occurred to him—his father's reputation could well place him on such a list. Salek's father was a logical target too.

He heard someone approaching. Not wanting to be seen reading the poster, he started to move on.

"Well, if it isn't the Jew boy," said Mende, overtaking him. "I see you've read our rules and are staying out of Aryan neighborhoods. That's wise. I would hate to have to blacken your other eye. But since you're being good, I won't have to, will I?"

Rudi managed to shake his head.

"I'll tell you what, Jew boy," Mende continued. "Since you are behaving yourself, I'm going to reward you. I'm going to let you shine my boots. They have gotten dirty walking through this neighborhood."

Rudi looked up, uncertain whether the German was serious or merely mocking him.

"Well, go on," urged Mende. "You know the rules. Surely you wouldn't want to be accused of being belligerent to a German soldier."

"I have nothing to shine shoes with," Rudi said.

"Of course, you do," the German told him. "Take off your coat."

Thinking again of the list that hung in the shop window, Rudi obeyed.

"Now your shirt," Mende demanded. "There—that nice soft shirt will be perfect for buffing my boots," he said, and he folded his arms and waited.

By this time Rudi felt nearly frozen. He stopped long enough to put his coat back on; then with the shirt in his hand he knelt at the German's feet.

"Go on," said Mende.

Slowly Rudi began to polish the man's boot.

"No, no, no," said Mende. "How do you expect to get any shine on them like that? You must first spit on them, then wipe them, spit on them again, and wipe them off. Repeat the process until they're so bright I can see my reflection in them. Now, go ahead. I'll tell you when to stop."

For more than an hour, Rudi knelt before Mende, spitting on his boots and wiping them with the shirt.

"I think they're clean enough," said Mende at last. Then he walked away.

Rudi's mouth was dry as dust, and he ached from kneeling on the cold stone street. He got up slowly. As he did, he caught a glimpse of his reflection in the window. He hardly recognized himself. He had not realized the damage Mende's blow had done. The whole side of his face was swollen, and there was a gash under his blackened eye. He stood several moments, looking at his disfigured

image. Why? Why had such a thing happened to him? Because he was a Jew.

He began to understand what Mrs. Serdusek had been trying to tell him. Here indeed was something unlike anything he had ever known. He looked down at the shirt he still held in his hand. It felt wretched, and so did he.

CHAPTER ELEVEN
THE CELEBRATION
NOV. 1939

Weeping may endure for a night, but joy cometh in the morning.

—Psalm 30:5

Rudi did not go by Salek's. He wanted to be alone. Nor did he intend to tell anyone about his incident with Mende, for the more he thought about it, the more he felt that there were some things that he would rather keep to himself.

He had hoped that the visits in the neighborhood would in some way cheer him. But again he was disappointed. By the time he returned home, he felt even more sullen.

"My," his father said, "I thought you looked just about as gloomy as any boy could possibly look when you left this morning. I see I was wrong."

Rudi tried to smile. "I didn't see anyone or anything that made me feel any better."

"From the looks of you, what you saw made you feel worse."

"It did." Rudi admitted. "Do you remember Mr. Androsky and his family?"

"Yes, why?"

"Well, you should see him now. You wouldn't even know him. I couldn't believe it when he answered the door. His face is all—well, bloated-like, and he has puffy bags under his eyes. And though his body's really skinny, his legs are so swollen he can hardly stand up. What's wrong with him, papa?"

"He's starving to death," his father said quietly.

"I guess that's what he was trying to explain to me," said Rudi.

"What did he tell you?"

"He said that he'd been able to get only two ration cards for his whole family."

"He has three children, doesn't he?"

"Yes," said Rudi. "He said his wife was sick too."

"I imagine she is in just about the same shape he is," said Dr. Kaplan. "They're probably giving any food they can get to the children. We'll have to do something. Maybe I can talk to Mr. Serdusek and get hold of one or two more cards."

"What if you can't?" asked Rudi.

"Then I'll save half of my food for them," he said.

"Me too," said Rudi.

"No," his father said. "You're growing too fast right now. I'm afraid if you eat any less, it won't be long until you show the same signs of malnutrition. Don't worry, son. I'll think of something. I can also get one or two bottles of Wigantol for them."

"What's that?" Rudi asked.

"Basically a tonic with a few vitamins—not many, but every little bit helps. These days vitamins are more precious than gold."

"That's not all I saw, papa," Rudi continued. "Over half the houses I went to had at least one person with typhoid—some more."

"I know. It's spreading like fire in a dry forest—especially in this part of town," his father said.

"It was hard enough to get medicine for it when you were working at the hospital. What're you going to do now?"

"I discovered while I was out that they have set up a small Jewish hospital out past Salek's house," his father told him.

"I heard about that, too," said Rudi. "But I also found out that nobody will go there. They're afraid to."

"Did anyone tell you why?" asked his father.

"The doctors make them stay in the hospital for treatment, and nobody wants to spend the night there," Rudi told him. "Mrs. Zyskind said that the Germans have raided the place three different nights and taken the patients off to work camps."

Rudi's father said nothing.

"Why would they do something so stupid, papa? It's obvious they're not going to get any work out of sick people."

"That's true," was all his father replied. Then he added, "Maybe I can get some of the medicine from the hospital to give to the patients here. Once we get a couple of rooms set up, I'll go see what I can do. But first—has it occurred to you yet what day it is?" his father asked.

Rudi sighed. "What difference does it make?"

"Not much, I guess," he said. "I must admit though, I didn't think I'd ever hear you say that."

"What are you talking about?" Rudi asked.

"Well, I just thought since you went to all that trouble to make sure you had your mother's letters, you'd at least remember when it was time to open one."

Rudi stopped. "It's my birthday!" he exclaimed.

His father laughed. "Very good. I was running out of hints."

"I can't believe it," Rudi said.

"Neither can I. I didn't think even a war could make a twelve-year-old forget his birthday."

"Where's the letter?" asked Rudi.

"Before I give it to you, I have one other surprise. Follow me," his father said, and he led Rudi over to the rickety table in the corner. There was a plate covered with a cloth napkin. His father snatched the napkin off the plate with a flourish.

"A sweet roll!"

"I suppose it would be more accurate to call it a sweet biscuit," his father told him. "It's a little small, but—"

"It's sweet," said Rudi. He scooped it up. "That's all that counts. Where in the world did you get it?"

"Mrs. Serdusek and I made a bargain. One of my former patients gave me a little coffee—at least it resembled coffee. You know how Mrs. Serdusek loves coffee, and I needed a sweet roll. We traded."

"It's great," said Rudi, stuffing it in his mouth.

His father grinned. "I see you forgot your manners along with your birthday. Maybe we could thank the Lord for it now."

"Sorry. I was just so hungry," said Rudi.

"I understand, and I am certain God does as well," he said. And they bowed their heads and prayed together.

As soon as they had finished praying, Dr. Kaplan took a letter from his shirt pocket and handed it to Rudi.

"While you read this, I'm going to scout around and see if I can find some rooms worth fixing up."

"Thanks, papa," Rudi said. "I'll come help in a few minutes."

"No rush," his father said as he left the room.

Although Rudi was eager to read the letter, he didn't want to open it too quickly. Taking time before reading it seemed to make having it even better, and he planned to enjoy the experience as long as he could.

It's amazing how much papa's been able to do with this place, he thought as he walked across the room. His father had even found some glass to repair the room's two broken windows, and Mrs. Serdusek had given them some scrap cloth to use as curtains. *Not such a bad place to have a birthday,* he said to himself as he pushed the cloth aside to let the sun come through the window and warm him. *If only it weren't so cold most of the time.* Then sitting up against the wall, he opened his letter.

for Nov. 15, 1939

Dear Rudi,

HAPPY BIRTHDAY! I trust by now you have enjoyed some birthday sweets and a time of celebration. Come to think of it, however, if your father hasn't improved his cooking over the years, you might do well to skip the "sweets" and be satisfied with the celebration. But then again, even if he hasn't learned to cook, I'm sure he's still very clever and that he's managed to figure out a way to get you some delicious birthday treat.

For the past few letters, I've concentrated on sharing several of the family's memories. But this time, I think I'd like to take you even further back to something a little more personal. It's a memory from my own childhood—a lesson I learned when I was very young and one that seemed to "grow up" with me over the years. Now that you're a little older, I think you'll understand why it means so much to me.

When I was small, I was terribly afraid of the dark. It was the first real problem I remember facing, and there seemed to be no explanation or remedy for it. Night after night, I would avoid going to bed, and once in bed my imagination would conjure up all sorts of terrifying scenes. I was sure that there were frightful things crawling under the bed or that there were horrid creatures lurking in the wardrobe. Of course, that seems very silly now, but it didn't seem so then. Anyway, one evening, when I was about six, my father and I were waiting for dinner. I was playing quietly while he was reading his Bible.

Suddenly he looked up from his reading. "You would like this verse, Ingrid," he said to me. "It tells you something about heaven that will make you very happy."

"What is that?" I asked, for by now he'd aroused my curiosity.

"It says in Revelation twenty-two verse five that 'there shall be no night there,' " he said, and he smiled down at me.

For the first time I understood something about what heaven would really be like. It would be a place where I would never be afraid, for to me "no night" meant no fear. From then on when I went to bed, I would try to imagine heaven. I would try to imagine what it would be like to live in a place without darkness. The thought so fascinated me that I forgot to be afraid.

But you know, Rudi, once I'd overcome that fear, I found that it was replaced by more "grown-up" worries. It seemed as I grew older that more and more events that I could not understand or control rose up before me. There were not only fears but frustrations and disappointments as well.

Still, no matter how the problems changed, I always found comfort in going back to the verse my father told me when I was six. It was as if every problem was in some measure like my nighttime fear, and I felt better if I reminded myself that "night" would someday vanish. Thus, my understanding of heaven broadened. "No night" meant more than freedom from fear. It meant no struggling with anger, no grappling with discouragement, and infinitely more.

I also began to realize that the verse had meaning for me in the present as well as the future. I began to see that just as "night" is part of this life, so is morning. No matter what the difficulty, it eventually passes just as surely as the sun comes up each day. You may not feel that way when you are in the middle of some problem. But trust me, son, it is so. And I have found that if I think of this truth at the very moment I am fearful, angry, or discouraged, it helps me see the situation clearly and gives me the strength to deal with it as I should. That's why I wanted to tell you about it, for surely you will soon be facing more "grown-up" problems. And I want very much to help you see things clearly. As your mother, I have sufficient faith in you to believe that once you see, you will be strong enough to face whatever comes.

Love,

Mother

Carefully Rudi folded his mother's letter. Then he closed his eyes for a few moments to think about the passing of night and the coming of morning.

CHAPTER TWELVE
THE HOSTAGES
NOV. 1939

Thus saith the Lord, Let not the wise man glory in his wisdom, neither let the mighty man glory in his might, . . . But let him that glorieth glory in this, that he understandeth and knoweth me, that I am the Lord which exercise lovingkindness, judgment, and righteousness, in the earth: for in these things I delight, saith the Lord.
—Jeremiah 9:23a-24

Rudi was startled from his thoughts when Salek burst into the room.

"Rudi! They've taken papa!"

Rudi felt a wave of fear come over him. "What are you talking about?"

"Just hurry—get your father!" Salek shouted. "We've got to get to the Council building before the soldiers take him away!"

Rudi rushed from the room with Salek right behind him. In moments they found Dr. Kaplan.

"The Germans have Mr. Serdusek!" Rudi shouted.

"Where?"

"They're holding him with about twenty other men at the Council Office," said Salek. "Please, hurry! They already have a truck waiting to take them."

Rudi's father quickly led the boys out into the street. "Where's your mother?" he asked Salek.

"She's already there," Salek told him.

"Why was your father at the Council building today?" Rudi asked as he and Salek ran along together in an effort to keep up with Dr. Kaplan's pace. "He isn't usually there on the Sabbath."

"One of the Council members stopped by the house and told him he had to come," Salek told him.

"Who?" Rudi's father asked.

"I don't know. I was upstairs when he came," said Salek. "I just know that it was someone who worked with papa. But it was a woman who came and told us that he was in trouble."

When they arrived, Rudi could see that SS officers were blocking the entrance of the building, while a crowd of women on the steps clamored for the release of their husbands. A few Poles had stopped, but only to watch. They made no effort to see whether they might be of help.

Rudi watched the soldiers push the women back from the door with their heavy sticks and rifle butts. "It doesn't look too good, papa," he whispered as he lifted his hand to his face and felt the gash beneath his eye.

His father made no comment on Rudi's observation but turned to Salek and simply said, "I'm going to try to find your mother, Salek." Then turning to Rudi he told him, "Whatever you do, make sure you don't get separated from me."

Rudi grabbed onto his father's jacket while Salek clutched Rudi's coat. But even with this precaution, Rudi found that it was difficult to stay close to his father while moving through the frantic crowd.

"There she is," he at last heard his father say.

Rudi refused to release his hold on his father's coat even after they had stopped.

"Sara—what's going on?" Rudi's father asked.

"Oh, Jakob, do something!" Mrs. Serdusek pleaded.

"I will, but first tell me what has happened."

"All I know is that early this afternoon one of the men from the Council came to the house. He said that the Gestapo had called a special meeting and that they insisted Eryk come here immediately. The next thing I knew, a woman was pounding on the door."

"She told us that the Germans might kill the Council members!" Salek broke in.

"She said they were threatening mass execution because the Jewish leaders had failed to carry out the Nazis' orders," Salek's mother continued. "I sent Salek after you because I didn't know what else to do, and I—"

Just then Rudi spotted someone coming out of the building. "Look, they're letting someone out!"

"I think it's the same man who came to the house," added Mrs. Serdusek.

The man was immediately encircled by women and children and bombarded with questions.

"What's he saying, papa?" asked Rudi.

"I don't know," his father said. "Let's move closer. I want to hear."

"Are they letting anybody else out, mama?" inquired Salek.

"Not that I can see," she said as she followed Dr. Kaplan's lead. By the time they were close enough to hear, the crowd had quieted and was anxiously listening to the one man who had been freed.

"I don't know what they intend to do with the hostages," Rudi heard the man say. "They've not made that clear."

"Where is my father? Where is Mr. Serdusek?" interrupted Salek.

"Your father's still inside, son. But he's fine, I assure you, he's fine."

"For how long, sir?" asked Salek's mother.

"I hope they will release them soon, Mrs. Serdusek," the man replied.

"If they plan to release them, why is that truck waiting here?" asked another woman.

"It could be just to frighten you," the man answered.

"Why'd they let you come out?" asked Rudi.

"I imagine they wanted me to do what I am trying to do right now—to let you know why they're holding the Council members hostage."

"They are holding them because you were stupid enough to come to our homes this afternoon and insist that the Council meet!" a woman shouted. Rudi turned toward her. He had never seen such fury in a woman, and her anger seemed to spark the same feelings in many of the others.

"Why in the world did you tell them to come here?" another said.

"Surely you knew something like this would happen," said still another.

"No, honestly—" the man tried to explain, but his voice was lost in the rising tumult.

"Quiet!" shouted Dr. Kaplan. "We can't decide what should be done until we know what's happened. Listen to him. Maybe then we can see our way clear to get them freed."

The crowd quieted, and Dr. Kaplan turned once again to the man. "Go on," he said.

"I finally rounded everyone up by 4:00. Honestly, I had no idea of what they wanted. They simply told me that every Council member must be present. Even after we'd assembled there was no clue. They gave no instructions. We sat there for at least an hour waiting."

"The fact that the Nazis had called Jews to a meeting should have been some clue." It was the same woman who had first shouted at the man.

"What would you have done?" he yelled back at her. "They told me that if I could not get the men to meet, they would hunt them down and kill them in their homes. Is that what you would have wanted?"

The woman made no reply, but Rudi could see that her fury seemed to cool somewhat. The man calmed himself and once again continued.

"About 5:00 several Gestapo officers burst into the room without warning and locked the door behind them. We all jumped up, but before we knew what was happening they'd encircled us. They were carrying rifles, whips, and pistols. For several minutes no one said a word. We all just stood there looking at them while they stared back at us. Finally, one of them—a man named Mende—spoke."

The very mention of Mende's name made Rudi's stomach turn.

"He addressed us as if we were common criminals," the man continued, "saying that from now on we were to carry out the *Führer's* wishes. He said that the fate of all the Jews was in our hands and that if we did not cooperate, his men would see to it that all the Jews in Warsaw were murdered."

Rudi looked at his friend standing beside him and remembered all that Salek had said about Germans shooting Jews. But it seemed that Salek now believed such a thing could never really happen—especially to his father. They might take his father away—which would be bad enough—but they would never shoot him. Rudi remembered Mende and did not doubt that they would— with delight. Rudi grasped his father's coat more tightly.

"What exactly are these orders that they refused to carry out?" Dr. Kaplan asked.

"They wanted us to demand that all the Jews move into one restricted area—a ghetto area that would be walled in."

"That doesn't sound like such a bad idea to me," said Rudi, for he wanted nothing more than a wall between himself and Mende.

"The boy's right," one woman seconded. "At least we would be kept away from the Germans."

"That's where you're wrong," the man said. "First of all, the area is so small that we could not all possibly live there. Secondly, do you really think they would leave us alone after they'd imprisoned us? Tell them," the man pleaded, turning to Dr. Kaplan for support.

"He's right," Rudi heard his father say. "It would mean that they would have us exactly where they want us."

"And that means," the man added, "that any time they want to destroy us, they could do it quickly and efficiently."

"So the Council's refusal to carry out that order was what brought on the threatened execution?" asked Dr. Kaplan.

"Yes—"

Rudi was so intent on listening to the conversation that he failed to notice that Salek had left his side until he turned to speak to him.

"Papa," Rudi interrupted, "where's Salek?" But before he had even finished the question, he spotted his friend. "Look, papa! Salek's trying to get in there!"

The man from the Council stopped.

"Salek!" Mrs. Serdusek cried. "Salek!"

"Wait here, Sara; I'll get him," said Dr. Kaplan. Then turning to Rudi he warned, "Don't you move."

Salek was trying to fight his way up the Council building stairs, but each time he went up one step, he was shoved back down by a soldier. He was no match for grown men, and Rudi could not believe that he kept on trying.

"I just want to see my father, please," Rudi heard him pleading.

"Try this way," said one soldier as he stepped aside. But as soon as Salek tried to pass, he shoved him down the stairs.

"Maybe he thinks he can get through here better," shouted another soldier.

By the time Dr. Kaplan reached him, the soldiers were making quite a sport out of shoving him around. Quickly Dr. Kaplan took hold of him.

"Oh, let him come, let him come," laughed the Germans.

"Salek," said Dr. Kaplan, turning him around. Rudi could see tears streaming down Salek's face.

"If I could just get to papa," Salek cried, "I would know what we should do."

"You're not helping matters," Dr. Kaplan told him. "Now come on. We're going back to your mother." He took him firmly by the hand. Salek submitted.

Just as Rudi's father turned Salek over to his mother, the crowd was distracted by a German military car driving up with several more officers—one of whom was Captain Franke. As the officers got out of the car and made their way toward the building, the man from the Council who had been speaking to them moved deeper into the crowd until he disappeared.

Captain Franke was weaving his way through the crowd when he spotted Dr. Kaplan. Changing his course, Franke made his way toward Rudi's father.

"Dr. Kaplan, I believe," he said when he had reached them. "Would you be so kind as to tell me what is going on here?"

"You should know," said one woman before Rudi's father could answer.

"Ah, Madame, that's where you're wrong," said Captain Franke calmly. "Even the military has its problems with communication. I did not order this gathering. That is why I'm here now." Then turning back to Dr. Kaplan, he continued. "Now, tell me who is in there and why. And then I will make my entrance."

"They have about twenty Jewish Council members in there, and they're threatening to kill them."

"I presume by 'they' you mean soldiers?" asked Captain Franke.

"Yes, I mean soldiers," replied Dr. Kaplan. "I only know the name of one—Mende—a name I'd like to forget," he said quietly.

"Yes," said Captain Franke, looking down at Rudi. "I imagine you would."

"Apparently the Council refused to comply with an order to establish a ghetto for Jews."

"A ghetto?" said Captain Franke quickly.

"Yes."

The Captain stood for several moments, and it appeared that the more he thought about Dr. Kaplan's words, the more agitated he became. At length he said, "And you say Mende is in there?"

"He is," said Dr. Kaplan.

At that moment the doors opened. The Council members were being led out and down the stairs in single file. Rudi saw Mr. Serdusek.

"There he is, Salek," said Rudi, pointing him out.

"Papa," Salek cried and ran toward him.

Hearing his son, Mr. Serdusek looked up but lost his footing and tripped on one of the steps. Immediately a soldier began to lash him with a whip.

"Eryk!" his wife cried out, but she was too frightened to move. Dr. Kaplan shoved the crowd aside and rushed to him. Mr. Serdusek was trying to get up, but the soldier's blows hindered him. Rudi's father pushed Salek out of the way and tried to shield Mr. Serdusek from the attack. When Rudi saw his father being lashed, he ran to them as well and was about to tear into the German when Captain Franke stepped in.

"Stop it!" he ordered the soldier.

The soldier, little more than a boy, looked up surprised, his hand still poised to strike another blow.

"Stop it, I said!" repeated Captain Franke.

The soldier obeyed, and Dr. Kaplan helped Salek's father to his feet. By this time, Mrs. Serdusek had joined them.

Mende emerged from the building. As soon as he saw Franke, he approached him. "We are taking a few of these Jews with us to insure that we get what we want out of the rest. They are very loyal to each other, you know," he said, looking at Mrs. Serdusek clinging to her husband. "Rather clever, don't you think?"

Captain Franke ignored Mende and turned to the soldier who had beaten Mr. Serdusek. "I do not want to see you lift that whip again. Is that clear?"

"Yes, sir," the young soldier replied.

"That goes for the rest of you as well," he said, addressing the other men. "I expect my soldiers to behave themselves as military men," he continued, "not as common, undisciplined rabble!" Then he turned toward Mende and said, "I will see you in my office—now." And without waiting for a reply, he turned and walked away.

Mende stood scowling until Franke's car drove out of sight. Then he shouted to the men. "Come on, let's get them into the truck."

Mr. Serdusek gently pushed his wife from him and turned to Dr. Kaplan. "Jakob—"

"Don't worry," Rudi's father assured him. "I will watch over Sara and Salek until your return."

Salek took his father's arm. "Papa, tell them something. Explain to them that—well, just say something to let them know they cannot take you away."

Mr. Serdusek gently forced Salek to release his hold and looking down on him said, "I—I can do nothing, son."

Salek looked as if he were uncertain that he had heard his father say such words. "But, papa, you said that you could reason with them—that you could find a way."

His father shook his head, and in a voice that Rudi barely heard, he said, "I was wrong."

Salek stood motionless, helplessly looking up into his father's face. Mr. Serdusek could not bear the look and turned to his wife. "I'm sorry, Sara," he said as they led him away.

Rudi's father put his arm around Mrs. Serdusek and drew Rudi and Salek to him as well. "We won't give up," he said. "There is still hope."

"Not for Jews, Jakob," Mrs. Serdusek replied. "No man will dare to help a Jew."

"I do not intend to rely on the help of men," said Rudi's father. "I will go to the God who created them."

"I'm afraid He, too, has forsaken us," said Mrs. Serdusek.

"You're wrong, Sara," was all that Rudi's father replied.

It was growing dark. Since no more could be done that day, Rudi and his father took Salek and Mrs. Serdusek home. They left them with the assurance that in the morning Dr. Kaplan would visit Gestapo headquarters and find out any information he could.

"Papa," said Rudi, once they arrived home safely, "I have always believed that God will hear me when I pray. But right now I'm not so sure. From the looks of things, it seems Mrs. Serdusek is right; maybe God has forsaken us. Maybe what people are saying is true—maybe He is angry with the Jews for putting Christ to death."

His father sat down at the table and motioned for Rudi to join him. "Rudi," he began, "Christ came to earth to die and rise again. No man or race of men took His life from Him; He laid it down for us—all of us—that we might live. We are all guilty before God for our sin, and for that sin Christ died. But He made that sacrifice willingly. People who accuse the Jews speak as if Christ's death were some unfortunate mistake. And that is foolishness."

"Then you really think that He still hears us—that He will hear us when we pray for Mr. Serdusek?" asked Rudi.

"Yes, I do," his father said. "I will go further, son, and say that this whole affair today may be the beginning of the answer to a prayer I have prayed for many years."

"What prayer?" asked Rudi.

"You know that for a long time I've tried to speak with Mr. Serdusek about Christ. He would never listen. That's been painful for me, Rudi, for Eryk Serdusek and I have been friends for years. As a matter of fact, when we were young, we were much like you and Salek," he said, smiling. "The only difference was that he was usually the one to lead us into all kinds of wild adventures. In yours and Salek's case, you are the one to do the leading.

"But did you see him today, Rudi, when he came out of that building?" his father asked as his smile faded.

"Yes," Rudi said. "It's the first time I have ever seen him look—I guess 'afraid.' "

"That's right. You see, he has always been a strong, self-sufficient man. But in that room today, I think he realized for the first time that there are things in life that he cannot master. And Rudi, that is a terrible blow for a man like Eryk Serdusek."

"I don't think it was too easy on Salek either," Rudi added.

"I know. But son, it is the first step toward realizing their true needs. I think that now Mr. Serdusek may be willing to admit that to be strong or wise or even 'good' is not enough to keep us from the perils of this life— or the next. Men need someone stronger, wiser, and better than themselves. They need Christ."

CHAPTER THIRTEEN
THE HOMECOMING
NOV. 1939

And fear not them which kill the body, but are not able to kill the soul: but rather fear him which is able to destroy both soul and body in hell.
—Matthew 10:28

Rudi stood at the Serduseks' window watching for his father, while Salek and his mother sat side by side on the sofa. There had been no conversation since Dr. Kaplan had gone, and that had been over an hour ago.

For the last five days Rudi's father had gone daily to the German military headquarters for information. The first three days the Germans refused even to speak with him. On the fourth day, however, he was granted an interview with Captain Franke for the following afternoon. Rudi, along with Salek and his mother, now waited anxiously for news.

Rudi prayed that they would hear something soon, because the uncertainty of the situation was becoming almost unbearable for him. He could not imagine what it must be like for Salek and Mrs. Serdusek.

"Here he comes!" Rudi said, running toward the door. Salek ran after him, and by the time Rudi had opened the door, Mrs. Serdusek was there as well.

"They will be free by evening," Dr. Kaplan said as he entered.

"Thank God!" cried Salek's mother.

"That is exactly what I think we ought to do," said Rudi's father. "Do you mind?" he asked, looking at Mrs. Serdusek.

She hesitated only a moment. "Of course not," she said, and she and Salek bowed their heads to pray with Rudi and his father.

When Dr. Kaplan finished praying, Salek took him by the hand. "Did you get to see him, Dr. Kaplan? Did they let you see him?"

"No," he answered, "but they assured me he was all right."

"What about the ghetto order?" asked Salek's mother.

Dr. Kaplan looked grave. "I don't know. I do know that there are some other orders in the works, and I imagine the Council will be expected to enforce them."

"What other orders?" asked Rudi.

"I'm not sure," his father told him. "We'll have to wait until Salek's father gets home. I'm sure they have let him know exactly what they expect."

"Let's go outside and wait for him," Salek suggested.

"I don't know how long it'll be before he gets here, Salek," Dr. Kaplan warned. "It could be thirty minutes or three hours, and it's pretty cold out there."

"I don't care," Salek said.

Rudi agreed. "Me either."

Rudi's father turned to Mrs. Serdusek. "What do you think, Sara?"

"I suppose it'll be all right," she said. "But both of you button your coats and keep your collars up about your necks."

"And stay right in front of the house," added Rudi's father. "I want to be able to see you if I should look out that window."

"Yes, sir," Rudi answered, for Salek was already out the door.

"I hope your father's really all right," said Rudi as soon as they had settled themselves on the stoop.

"He'll be fine," Salek told him. "I knew that he could think of something to make them let him go."

"I know how smart your father is, Salek," said Rudi, "but I don't think that the Nazis listen to anybody. I think God was the one who made them let him go."

Salek looked at Rudi for a moment. "Maybe," he admitted. "Still, papa's always been really good at handling people."

Rudi sighed and said no more.

A light snow began to fall. Rudi took his hand from his pocket and held it out to catch the soft white flakes. They drifted slowly down and settled lightly in the palm of his hand, for a moment—only a moment—then they disappeared. How quickly they vanished. *How quickly everything vanishes these days,* thought Rudi. He could be sure of nothing anymore—well, almost nothing. He was sure that his father would do all in his power to protect him. Still, maybe his father—like Salek's—would not be able to do enough.

For the first time, he realized that he, Rudi Kaplan, might not live to see the end of this horrid war. It was a strange thought, one he had never considered before. Oh, he had been afraid of being hurt, but he had never thought of dying—until now.

His mind turned again to the young trumpeter of Krakow, and he felt at that moment as if he, like the young boy in the story, were sitting against a tower wall, waiting for the dreaded hour to pass. Then he remembered his mother. There was comfort in that thought, for she had gone before him. She was waiting.

But what of Salek? Rudi had always believed that there was plenty of time for Salek to understand that Christ was the Jewish Messiah, plenty of time for him to believe in Christ as Saviour; after all, they were just kids. Now he was not so sure.

"Salek," he said, turning to his friend.

But at that moment Salek stood up. "Look, Rudi, I see someone coming!"

Rudi stood up as well to gaze into the distance. There was indeed someone coming, but it didn't look like Mr. Serdusek to Rudi. "That's not him, Salek," Rudi said. "He's not as tall as your father."

"I guess you're right." Disappointed, Salek sat back down on the steps.

Rudi stood studying the shadowy figure in the twilight. The man's face was not visible because he was bent forward, his chin nearly resting on his chest. He looked as if every muscle were weighted with some unseen burden. He walked, but there was no life in him.

The closer he came, however, the more uncertain Rudi felt. "Maybe I was wrong," he said after some thought. "Maybe it is your father. It looks like the hat and coat he wears."

"Let's run and see," said Salek, getting up again and moving down the steps.

"No, wait," said Rudi, going after him and taking his arm. "You heard my father. We can't go any farther than the front steps. He's coming closer now. We'll see in a minute."

The man was almost to them. "No," Salek said in a low tone. "That can't be papa."

"But his coat and hat—" Rudi protested.

The man heard the boys and looked up as if he had been startled from deep thought. It was Mr. Serdusek.

He stared at them a moment, then said, "Salek, you— you've forgotten your hat." His voice was hoarse and low, and he spoke in a distracted tone. He acted as if he had just gone out on an errand and upon returning noticed Salek's carelessness by chance. "You'll catch your death of cold, boy," he continued, his voice growing more firm. Then he passed them and started moving up the stairs.

His appearance and manner had so surprised them that neither Rudi nor Salek was able to utter a word.

Mr. Serdusek stopped on the steps as if remembering something, then he turned back to face them. "Here, take mine, son," he said, as he removed his hat and held it out to Salek.

Rudi almost gasped, for Mr. Serdusek's coal black hair was now as white as the falling snow.

"Papa!" said Salek, coming out of his stupor and running to his father.

Rudi was completely astonished by what he saw, and it was not until Mrs. Serdusek opened the door that he could pull himself together.

"Eryk," said Mrs. Serdusek in a voice that was no more than a whisper.

Mr. Serdusek turned to face her, but said nothing.

"Come in, Eryk," Dr. Kaplan said, and stepping past Mrs. Serdusek, he took Salek's father by the arm. "I think some soup might do him good," he said to Mrs. Serdusek. "He's had a long walk, and who knows when he last had anything to eat. Do you have some?"

"Yes, a bit," she told him.

Rudi's father and the Serduseks moved inside the house, but Rudi did not follow. Instead, he stood at the bottom of the steps, trying to imagine what could have happened to Mr. Serdusek to cause such a drastic change in him. Just five days, and his hair had turned completely white. After several moments, however, Rudi decided that maybe it was best not to think about it—maybe he didn't really want to know. He followed the others into the house.

Mrs. Serdusek had given her husband some soup and bread. She also prepared a bit of coffee for him. The food revived him somewhat, and in an hour or so, he seemed more like himself. But even after he'd begun to regain some strength and to talk more freely, he still sat rigid in his chair as if he were afraid that any moment he might have to run.

"They are no longer forcing the idea of a Jewish ghetto," he said. "At least, they are postponing it."

"Why?" asked Dr. Kaplan.

Rudi sensed in that one word his father's apprehension that the ghetto order might be replaced with something worse.

"It seems that the military and the SS cannot agree on who should be governing us," Mr. Serdusek replied. "To prove their power, the military refuse to enforce the SS's command. To them it is a simple matter of who is boss. Franke is military, but Mende—that devil of a man— is part of the SS, Hitler's elite fighting force."

"Like the Gestapo?" Dr. Kaplan asked.

"Yes. Many of them have never been soldiers, and the military resent them. So there's conflict."

"That conflict may be to our advantage," Dr. Kaplan said.

"I doubt that it will last," said Mr. Serdusek resignedly. "From what I have seen, I think we would fare better under the German military, but I am afraid it's only a matter of time before they give in to the SS."

"What will you do when that happens?" asked Mrs. Serdusek. Her husband did not answer.

"So," said Mrs. Serdusek quietly, "it is just a matter of time before we are all made captives."

Mr. Serdusek remained silent, and his silence convinced Rudi that Salek's mother was right.

"What else did you find out?" Dr. Kaplan asked.

Mr. Serdusek started to speak but then hesitated.

"Tell us, Eryk," urged Mrs. Serdusek.

Mr. Serdusek turned to Rudi's father. "They mentioned you, Jakob," he said.

"Mentioned me? What do you mean?" Dr. Kaplan asked.

"They said they would be visiting you in a day or two," continued Mr. Serdusek. "They—"

"What for?" Rudi interrupted, getting up from his seat. His father motioned for him to sit back down and wait for Mr. Serdusek to finish. He obeyed reluctantly.

"They know that you have started treating patients on your own," said Mr. Serdusek.

"And they object to that?" asked Rudi's father.

"No—not exactly," answered Mr. Serdusek. "They do say, however, that they want you to use standard procedures in your treatment."

"Standard procedures," laughed Rudi's father. "I have not been able to use 'standard procedures' since this war started."

"What they said was that they want you to begin treating your patients as they are now treated in the Jewish hospital here in the neighborhood."

Rudi's father said nothing. So Rudi spoke up. "People are afraid to go to that hospital. Why should papa do as they do?"

"What exactly are they referring to?" asked Dr. Kaplan. "Did they say?"

"Yes. They referred specifically to the treatment of typhoid patients. They want you to begin giving your patients the same drug that the other Jewish doctors use. I—I don't remember what it's called."

"Uliron?"

"Yes, that's it. The Germans have been providing it for the hospital staff. They are willing to provide it for you to use as well."

Rudi watched his father and could see that he was troubled—though he could not understand why. They had not been able to get any medicine at all. At least the Germans were apparently willing to provide something.

After several moments Mr. Serdusek spoke again. "You know that you must do as they say, Jakob?"

"No, I can't and I won't," Rudi's father replied.

"You haven't any choice," said Mr. Serdusek.

"You're right—I have no choice," Dr. Kaplan said. "I cannot kill innocent people."

The words startled Rudi. "Kill them?"

Mr. Serdusek protested. "They said that it was medicine—maybe not the best, but—"

"Yes, it is medicine, but to give it to a person with typhoid is deadly."

"But—Jewish doctors are giving it at the Jewish hospital," said Mr. Serdusek. "Surely—"

"I visited the hospital about three days ago," interrupted Rudi's father. "As a matter of fact, I was on my way home from the military headquarters, where I had tried unsuccessfully to get information about you, Eryk. At any rate, I saw what happens to the patients who received the drug you speak of. They die. They die very shortly after receiving their 'treatment.' "

"Maybe the doctors do not know," said Mrs. Serdusek.

"They know. They give the drug because the Nazis have threatened to arrest them if they do not. Of course, there are a few who will not follow the orders. But I assure you, they suffer for refusing."

"How could they—" gasped Mrs. Serdusek, and she got up and left the room.

"How can they do that, papa?" Rudi exclaimed in astonishment.

"They rationalize their deed by saying that the patient will die anyway," his father explained. "If he dies a little sooner, they say it does no harm. As a matter of fact, they have convinced themselves that it does great good. After all, there is one less mouth to feed. The Jewish rations will go further; thus, they can save others from starving."

"It does seem reasonable," said Mr. Serdusek. "After all, this is a war, and if things keep on as they are, none of us will live to see the end of it. We will either starve or be killed."

"It may be reasonable, Eryk, but it is not right," Dr. Kaplan said. "Right and wrong don't change because of crisis."

Rudi watched as Mr. Serdusek studied his father closely. "I'm afraid for you, Jakob," he finally said.

"And I for you," said Dr. Kaplan.

Mr. Serdusek shook his head. "I am free for the moment. But you—"

"Are you really?" asked Dr. Kaplan. "It seems to me that you are held captive by fear. Is that freedom?"

"You don't understand, Jakob," said Mr. Serdusek, growing more animated. "You don't understand these Germans. I do—now. And I'm telling you, we must do as they say. If you do not comply, they will send you off to a work camp. You may survive such a place, but I assure you, Rudi would not. Don't you see, I cannot protect you anymore. I cannot even protect my family!"

"I wouldn't ask you to protect me," said Dr. Kaplan. "Sometimes I think that you still believe we are children. Back then you often protected me, and I was grateful then— as now—for your friendship. But we are men now, Eryk, and to be frank, you are in greater need of protection than I am. The worst that they can do to me is kill me."

"I would say that that is quite enough."

"Yes, you would. That is the difference between you and me. I'm not afraid to die, for I'm assured of life after death, assured that I will go to be with the God who created me. And I am grateful that Rudi has that same assurance. But you and your family, Eryk, have no such security."

Mr. Serdusek sat staring at the floor. He did not respond, but neither did he try to change the topic of conversation. Salek watched his father closely.

"If you desire to protect those you love in the midst of this horror, you must look to something—Someone— outside of yourself."

"To Christ?" Mr. Serdusek asked.

"Yes, to Christ," said Dr. Kaplan.

"I have spent my life, Jakob, taking care of myself and my loved ones."

"And you have always been successful in doing so, but what about now?" asked Dr. Kaplan. "Do you honestly believe that by giving in to the Nazis you will be able to protect your family?"

"Still," said Mr. Serdusek, "I have never been able to believe in Christ as a Messiah. How can I believe now?"

"You can begin by listening to me," said Dr. Kaplan. "We have trusted each other for years. Can't you trust me now? Let me show you from the Law and the Prophets that Christ is God's promised one. Just listen, Eryk, if not for your own sake, for the sake of Sara and Salek. If there is a Messiah who can provide eternal life for us, should your wife and son not be given the chance to believe?"

Mr. Serdusek got up and left the room, but he returned only moments later. He was carrying a beautifully gilded but dusty copy of the Old Testament. His wife was by his side. Handing the book to Dr. Kaplan, he said, "Show me."

Rudi's father opened it to Isaiah and began to read. " 'Surely he hath borne our griefs, and carried our sorrows: yet we did esteem him stricken, smitten of God, and afflicted. But he was wounded for our transgressions, he was bruised for our iniquities: the chastisement of our peace was upon him; and with his stripes we are healed.' "

Rudi studied the Serduseks and was relieved to see that for the first time, Mr. and Mrs. Serdusek were indeed listening. And Salek was listening too.

CHAPTER FOURTEEN
THE SACRIFICE
NOV. 1939

Take now thy son, thine only son . . . whom thou lovest.
—Genesis 22:2a

A week had passed since Mr. Serdusek's homecoming. It had been a good week, for after that initial conversation, Rudi's father was able to talk freely to the Serduseks about Christ. For several days they all met together in the late afternoon to study and to talk about the prophecies in the Old Testament. Dr. Kaplan showed them passage after passage foreshadowing Christ as the Messiah. After so many years of prayer, it seemed to Rudi that Mr. Serdusek's heart was at last softening. Yes, it had been a good week—until today.

That afternoon the Gestapo had paid his father a visit and had given him their ultimatum: he was to treat all typhoid patients with the "standard" medication—uliron. Dr. Kaplan refused. Although the Germans did not openly threaten him, their visit aroused Rudi's deepest fears. It cast a shroud of sorrow over his father that seemed to blot out the joys of the previous week. Now it was well into the night, and Rudi could not sleep.

He lay on the sofa in a dark corner of the room and watched his father, who was sitting at the table, hovering over his Bible. The flame from the lantern on the table made the frost of his breath barely visible and threw fanciful shapes upon the wall. At the same time, however, Rudi noticed that it cast harsh shadows across his father's face, making him look worn and solemn.

Dr. Kaplan looked up from his Bible and gazed for several minutes into the lantern's flame. Then he stood up and with a decisive air made his way across the room to the sofa where Rudi lay.

"Rudi," he said quietly.

Rudi did not answer, for he felt that his father intended to tell him something he did not want to hear.

"Rudi," his father repeated, "are you awake, son?"

"Yes," Rudi finally admitted.

"We have to talk," his father said, as he placed his hand gently on Rudi's shoulder.

Rudi got up slowly, buttoned his coat, and followed him to the lighted corner of the room.

"Sit down, son," his father began. "I have something to tell you that is difficult for me to say." He stopped and looked down.

After several moments he continued, but still he did not look up. "I think you know already that the Nazis will be back for me. I can't do anything to avoid them, but I can see to it that you are out of their reach. I—"

"If they take you, they will have to take me too," Rudi said doggedly.

His father's voice was quiet. "No, son. You cannot come with me."

The words shot through Rudi like an arrow. "But I have to go with you," he protested, "I have to!"

His father looked up, and as the light fell across his face, Rudi could see the tears glistening in his eyes. He had never seen his father cry, and the very sight also made his eyes well up with tears.

"Rudi," Dr. Kaplan continued, "I have heard reports about the place where they will send me. Many believe the reports are exaggerated, and a few weeks ago I might have believed so too. But since that time I have seen what the Nazis are capable of—" He hesitated. "I'm afraid you couldn't survive such a place."

"Yes I could," Rudi argued.

His father's voice took the tone of reasoning. "Even if that were true, do you think they'd let us stay together once they got us to the camp? No, I assure you they would not. That's why I have spent hours this past week praying, asking God to show me what I ought to do. And He has. He has given me a promise—a promise that if I let you go, He will keep you."

"Go?" asked Rudi. "What do you mean?"

"I mean that you will have to leave here—to get away before the Germans come back for me."

"But where, papa?" cried Rudi. "Where am I to go?"

"Into the forest," said his father.

Rudi stared at him in disbelief.

"I have a plan," Rudi's father continued before Rudi could offer any argument. "I've talked with a friend of mine, a former patient. His brother, Oscar, was one of many who has managed to escape into the forest and join a resistance group there. He's been in contact with him, and he told me that Oscar will be able to help you. He's already been notified that you are coming."

Rudi tried desperately to think of some argument that would change his father's mind, but before he could do so, his father pulled out a carefully drawn map from his trousers pocket and went on.

"Our first job is to get you out of the city. I have spent the last few days finding an escape route for you.

There is one—only one, from what I can tell. It is here," he said, pointing to a spot on the map, "very close to the place where we dug the trenches with Salek and his father. You remember?"

"Yes, but—"

His father dared not hesitate. "By taking these back streets," he said, carefully going over each step, "you can reach that entrance. When you arrive, look for this place in the barbed-wire fence that the Nazis have erected—right about here—just this side of where we were digging that morning. You will find that the bottom wire is loose enough for you to lift it up and slide under. Of course, you must wait until the guard has turned his back—and you must be quick about it. I have watched other children go in and out this way. They escape daily into the fields in search of food and return just as it is getting dark. An adult could never get under the wire; that's why the Germans haven't noticed it. But you must be careful, Rudi." His father's voice was earnest.

"I'm not going, papa," Rudi said. "I'm not leaving you."

His father sat for a long while, staring down at the map before he finally spoke again.

"Rudi, I want to tell you something, something I've never told anyone else. And I don't know if I would have ever told you, had we not been brought to this place. But it may help you understand or at least have faith enough to accept what I am saying."

"Nothing could—"

"Just listen for a moment," his father interrupted. "It's—it's about your mother's death."

Rudi quieted, for it was the first time his father had actually mentioned his mother's death. Though his father often talked about her, it always seemed to Rudi that he spoke as if she had merely taken a journey and was soon to return.

"You see, Rudi," he began, "you're not the only one who has ever had to accept by faith what you could not understand. It was very difficult for me to lose your mother. When I learned that she was dying, my first reaction was fear. I could not imagine going on without her; nor could I imagine rearing you all by myself. You were so small and helpless, and I was—well, so clumsy.

"After the initial shock, however, I grew angry. I was angry with myself because I—a doctor—could do nothing to help the person I loved more than anyone else in the world. And I was angry with God as well. Surely, I reasoned, if He loved us, He would not make us suffer so.

"I am ashamed to say this, but I grew more bitter as she grew weaker. Of course, I hid it from her, for she continued to trust in God all through her illness, and my lack of faith would have hurt her deeply.

"When she died, I almost despaired. The only thing that kept me going was my love for you. You needed me, Rudi, and I couldn't let you down. In His mercy God began to work on me, to heal the hurt I felt and to bring me close to Him again.

"But even after I'd accepted His will for us and had begun to trust Him once again, I still did not understand—until two months ago on the night the Germans evicted us from our apartment. As I stood before your window and watched Mrs. Kaminsky's children and husband being torn from her—I understood that God had taken your mother home because He loved her. You see, son, your mother was very strong, but she had two weak points—you and me. Your mother was a Gentile, and eventually she would have faced the same horror Mrs. Kaminsky faced. Rudi, to lose us in such a manner would have been far more painful for her than any illness. I can now say that I am glad to know that she's in God's presence; I am grateful that I shall never be forced to leave her in the hands of Nazis."

"It seems that He could have waited a little longer before taking her," said Rudi.

"No, son. The Lord knew that I needed several years to grow without her, several years before I had the faith to face what I face now."

"Please, papa—" pleaded Rudi.

"I know you are young, Rudi, and I know that you have not lived long enough to look back and see God's hand in circumstances. Still, you do know that I love you as much as any father could, and that I would never ask you to do such a hard thing if I were not absolutely certain God is in it—absolutely certain that it's the right thing to do."

"I can't—I just can't go alone."

"Yes, yes you can. Any boy who is clever enough to execute a plan like you did in returning to our old apartment can carry out this plan as well."

"That was different," said Rudi.

"Yes, in many ways it was much more dangerous— and it was unnecessary. This time it is necessary."

Rudi knew that his father was waiting for some word of assurance from him, but he could not bring himself to offer any.

"Please, Rudi, please trust me," his father begged. "Trust me as I must trust my heavenly Father. I promise you—as He has promised me—if you go, you will see the end of this war."

"But what about you, papa?" Rudi asked desperately.

"I don't know. All that I can promise you is that we will see each other again—if not in this life, then in the next. But here, Rudi, is the promise God has given me to assure me of your safety." He turned his Bible toward Rudi and pointed to the verse. "Let's read it together."

Rudi looked down, but try as he would, he could not focus on the words. " 'He that dwelleth in the secret place of the most High shall abide under the shadow of the Almighty,' " he heard his father say. "The forest is God's secret place for you, Rudi. There—there you shall be under His shadow, where you will be safe. Please, son, please don't let me down."

"When must I go?" Rudi finally managed to say.

"As soon as we can get you ready," Dr. Kaplan told him.

Rudi ran to his father and threw his arms about him. And burying his face in his father's chest, he wished with all his heart that he could stay there until the darkness was past.

Child
of the
Forest

CHAPTER FIFTEEN
THE SECRET PLACE
NOV. 1939

Trust in the Lord with all thine heart; and lean not unto thine own understanding.

—Proverbs 3:5

Crouching down, Rudi pressed himself against the cold stone wall of a building. It was the last stronghold he could cling to, for he had reached the outskirts of the city. He knew that about fifty yards before him was the Germans' watchtower. Beyond that lay the open country, then the forest.

At first when he peered into the distant darkness, he could see only the tops of the tallest forest trees. Outlined in the moonlight, they looked as if they had been traced in silver on a deep blue velvet sky. And for a moment as he gazed on them, he forgot his fears. But then the searchlight from the Nazis' watchtower turned on its rotation. The harsh white beam cut through the darkness, accenting the tiny spikes in the barbed wire and making the two guards look almost ghostlike as they moved with the light along the fence.

Rudi re-created in his mind the map his father had drawn for him, and with his eyes he followed the soldiers' path until he came to the point of escape. It was just as his father had said: the wire was sagging.

Making it to the fence and getting under that wire were not going to be easy. He sat for several minutes, trying to think through his actions. He would have to calculate exactly the time it would take and the spot he was aiming for, and he would have to do it in pitch dark.

After studying the path of the light, he decided that it passed the desired spot about every sixty seconds. He was not at all sure that he could run the fifty yards to the fence and slide under the wire in the time he had.

He then turned over the possibility of running halfway on one rotation and completing his escape on a second rotation. It was possible that the tall grass could hide his figure from the beam if he managed to get out of its most direct light. But he was not sure of that either. The more he thought about it, the more he believed that it was best to try to make it all at once.

The night was cold, but he found that he was sweating. He wanted to tear his coat off, but he knew that would be foolish. So he sat there—sweating, waiting, watching— as the searchlight made its round several more times.

Reminding himself of God's promise to his father, he at last gained the courage to dart out into the darkness. As he did so, he felt as if his body were moving without his guidance, as if he were still leaning back against the wall, watching himself run forward.

He glanced to his right. The light seemed to be coming much faster than he had thought it would. When he finally reached his destination, he stretched out his hand and grasped the wire. It was taut. Frantically, he ran his fingers along the fence until he felt the wire sag.

By this time the light had already passed the halfway mark. He scrambled to the point of escape, and lifting the wire over his head, he slid beneath it. He had only to bring his left leg out from under the fence when something caught. He pulled and pulled, but the leg of his trousers seemed hopelessly entangled in the barbed wire. He gave one last yank. As he did, he felt tiny spikes tear his flesh; then he was free. He lifted his legs and rolled himself over just before the searchlight reached him.

Burying his face in the cold, wet grass, he waited. It seemed as if he could feel the heat from the light hovering over him, and he dared not look up. If he were to be shot, he did not want to see the bullet coming. He listened for gunfire, but the only thing he heard was the pounding of his heart and his own rapid breathing.

He did not know how long it was before he gained the courage to turn his head to one side. When he did, he saw that the light had passed him at least once, and was already coming toward him again. He lay very still. But this time, he turned his face to the ground only long enough for the light to pass over him. As soon as he was covered once again in darkness, he began moving away from the fence and out into the field, keeping as close to the ground as he could.

Grabbing hold of a clump of grass with his right hand, he pulled his left knee up and pushed himself forward. He then reached out with his left hand to clutch the grass and pulled his right leg up. Again and again he thrust himself forward until the muscles in his arms and legs began to stiffen. But in spite of the pain, he knew he could not stop. He had to keep moving straight ahead; he had to make it to the dirt road. Only then would it be safe to stand. Thus, he continued—left right, left right, left right.

It was at least thirty minutes before his hand reached out and touched hard earth. He tried standing but found that his muscles immediately rebelled, and he was forced to sit back down for a few moments. After rubbing his thighs and shoulders almost savagely, he managed to ease the cramping, and he tried standing up once more. He still ached all over, but he could walk.

Glancing back toward the city, he saw that the beam from the searchlight was only faintly visible. At last he was well away from the Nazi watchtower and its light. The forest lay just ahead.

As he began walking, he noticed that the soft twilight that covers the world just before dawn had settled on the fields and wrapped itself about the forest trees. He slowed his pace, for the closer he came to the forest the more reluctant he was to enter. He decided that once he had reached its edge, he would sit down and watch the sunrise. After all, Oscar had refused to set a definite time for their rendezvous. He said only that he would meet Rudi at the appointed place "sometime before nightfall." There was no need to hurry.

Minutes later he was leaning against the knotty trunk of an enormous tree. He looked down at his leg. It was still bleeding, but the cuts were not deep. Cupping his hand, he scooped up a clump of snow that had settled on one of the scrubby bushes next to him and pressed it against the wound. As the snow melted, it took away the sting. He then took out the knife his father had given him and cut a piece of cloth from his ragged pants leg and wrapped it tightly about the cut.

Once his leg was bandaged, he relaxed, and leaning back against the tree, he looked up. By now there were streaks of purple, orange, and gold splashed against the grayed horizon.

If only he could hold this moment, this moment full of color and quiet. It was very, very quiet. There were no sirens, no guns, no cracking whips, no weeping. The only sound was the soft creaking of young trees bending in the winter wind.

His thoughts turned to his father, and he wondered whether the Nazis had returned for him. If so, he knew that they would have come just before sunrise. They always did.

It occurred to him that the truck taking the prisoners to work camps would have to pass on the road before him. It would be soon. He decided to wait and see whether his father were indeed one of the prisoners on the truck. If he were not? Well, perhaps—perhaps he would go back.

The morning sun was growing brighter. Thus Rudi decided that it might be better if he moved back behind some of the trees. He did not really know if or when the Germans ventured out beyond their watch, and there was no sense in taking chances. Besides, since he was not that far from the road, he would be able to hear the truck approaching.

He had barely taken up his new post when he heard the familiar rumbling. He stepped out cautiously and crouched down. The truck was still quite a way off. But even from a distance he could see that, unlike the other trucks he had seen, this one was not open; it had a canvas covering. It would be impossible to see all—if any—of the prisoners. Still, he determined that he would try.

How laboriously it moved over the dirt road. It seemed ages before it was close enough for him to see clearly. When at last it was near enough, Rudi noticed that the canvas was not securely tied. As the covering flapped carelessly in the wind, it looked to Rudi as if all the men and women were huddled together on the floor of the truck trying to stay warm—all except one. Rudi recognized his father's lanky frame standing at the very back of the truck. He was holding on to one of the curved bars over which the canvas was draped. His face was calm, and though he did not look toward the forest, it seemed to Rudi that he knew his son was watching.

The truck passed slowly, but not slowly enough for Rudi. He rushed from tree to tree, unwilling to let it out of his sight. But soon he stopped running, for he realized that it was useless to do so. He had to admit to himself that there was no turning back, and the thought made him feel lonelier than he had ever felt before.

Reaching inside his coat and down inside his sweater, he ran his fingers across his mother's letters. *This war can't last forever,* he reminded himself. Then his father's words came back to him: "You must trust me, Rudi, just as I must trust my heavenly Father. Please, son, please don't let me down."

"I won't, papa," he said aloud in an effort to stir up his courage. Then he turned and walked into the forest.

CHAPTER SIXTEEN
THE CHASE
NOV. 1939

And the hand of our God was upon us, and he delivered us from the hand of the enemy, and of such as lay in wait by the way.

—Ezra 8:31b

Rudi's father had instructed him to go to the place of rendezvous as quickly as possible and wait. So, determining to put everything else from his mind, he pulled the instructions he had been given out of his pocket and looked them over carefully.

From what he could tell, he would find his initial clue close to the place where he had watched the sunrise, for he had been told to take the most direct path from the point of escape to the edge of the woods. From this point he was to continue moving straight into the forest until he found a red woolen scarf tied to a low-hanging branch. If the scarf was knotted, he was to go to the left. If it was merely wrapped once about the branch, he was to go to the right. He would find a second tree in one of these two directions.

The second tree, as well as the succeeding trees, was to be marked by a small arrow etched into the bark near the ground. The arrows would indicate his direction. By following this path of trees, he would eventually reach the meeting place, located on the bank of a river.

The fact that his final destination was a riverbank troubled Rudi slightly, for he knew that the Vistula had several tributaries running through the surrounding forests. He feared the possibility of ending up on the wrong bank. *But if I'm careful,* he assured himself, *I'll find it.*

He tucked the instructions back inside his pocket and set out. He found the scarf with little difficulty. Relieved, he untied the knot, turned to the left, and continued his search.

Locating the next clue took more time. An arrow mark was a lot harder to spot than a bright woolen scarf. But he finally found the sign on the gnarled root of an old tree. Had he not tripped on the root which was jutting up from the ground, he might not have found it at all, for he had already examined that particular tree carefully— or so he had thought. The arrow pointed straight ahead. *I've got to be more careful,* he told himself as he moved on.

After an hour or more, Rudi noticed that his travel was becoming more difficult. He was moving deeper into the forest where the trees and bushes were more numerous. The undergrowth was growing thicker, too, making it harder to forge a decent path for walking.

He stopped momentarily to rest. As he did, an abrupt sound startled him. It was a sharp, cracking sound, as if someone had suddenly broken a sturdy branch across his knee. Rudi looked in the direction from which the sound had come. He saw nothing.

Perhaps Oscar has decided to come and find me, he thought. The thought, however, did not comfort him, and an eerie feeling came over him as he resumed his search.

His fear began to urge him on until he was nearly running. Branches started to lash and scratch his face, and the thick undergrowth reached out—as if it were some living thing—to snatch at his trousers and grab hold of his feet. His panic was rising to a dangerous pitch when he stopped. *Keep your head!* he scolded himself. He had already gotten too far from the last marked tree. So he doubled back, slowly.

When he again heard his pursuer, he did not immediately stop or turn around. Instead he slowed his pace, shoved his hands into his pockets, and kicked some leaves about as if he were curious to see what lay beneath them. He also took the red scarf out of his coat pocket and wrapped it about his neck. Then looking up nonchalantly, he scanned the area. The sounds stopped.

It's not Oscar, he reasoned. *He would have recognized the scarf and identified himself. But it can't be a German either. Why would a German want to hide in the woods?*

After several minutes of such reasoning, his fear was replaced with a sense of irritation. He wanted to get to his destination, but he was not going to take just anyone along with him. Leaning up against one of the trees, he decided to wait it out until whoever it was showed himself or moved on. Rudi had time. Besides, he had no objection to taking another few minutes of rest.

His patience paid off. After about thirty minutes he heard a distinct rustling in the brush about 100 feet to his right. Maintaining his uninterested air, he turned his head in the direction of the sound. Whoever it was stopped for a moment and then began moving again—this time *away* from Rudi. The sounds grew fainter and fainter until they faded out completely. Rudi stayed put for another hour, listening for any sign of return. Hearing nothing, he continued.

But he had not been moving more than forty-five minutes, when he found he was being followed again. This time he was determined to discover who was trailing him.

Spotting a large tree with several low, drooping branches, he moved toward it quickly. He hoisted himself up into the tree and kept climbing until he had reached a good height. Then he settled himself securely on one of the branches.

At first he could see nothing as he looked down into the trackless undergrowth. Then the crackling of twigs drew his attention, and he spotted someone moving through the brush.

Rudi kept his eyes riveted on the figure until the man came clearly into view. Though his ragged clothes hung loosely on his frame, Rudi could see that he was by no means frail. He was large-boned and muscular. He had thick yellow tufts of hair that stuck out from under his cap in all directions and a drooping mustache that curved down around his mouth like an angry frown until it disappeared into his matted beard.

There was a wild look about him, and as Rudi watched him creeping forward, he thought of a story he once read about a panther hunting prey. The longer Rudi looked down on his pursuer, the more he prayed that he was well hidden.

The man moved very slowly, carefully studying the ground before him. He continued until he was directly under Rudi's tree. There he stopped.

Maybe he didn't see me climb the tree, thought Rudi.

In his fright, Rudi had unconsciously been holding his breath, and he did not notice it until his lungs felt like they were at the point of bursting. Realizing that he had to release the pent-up air, he began to exhale, trying not to gasp the air out all at once. But his efforts were not good enough. Immediately the man cocked his head as if he had heard something. Rudi stopped and tried to hold it in once more, but it was no use. He had to breathe. The man looked up, lifting his rifle as he did so.

"You," he called out roughly, keeping his gun aimed up in the tree. "Come on down."

Rudi waited.

"I know somebody's up there, and I'll give you to the count of ten to start moving down," the man said in a more threatening tone.

Rudi hesitated.

"One, two, three," the man began counting.

Deciding that he'd rather take his chances on the ground, Rudi began his descent, stepping carefully from limb to limb.

"Not a bad climber," said the man, lowering his gun only slightly. It was in a less threatening, but still dangerous, position.

Rudi looked squarely at the man but said nothing.

The man returned Rudi's gaze with a stony stare; then suddenly he lifted his hand and reached for Rudi's neck. Rudi jumped aside, and for a moment he did not know whether he should bolt into the woods or try to fight.

"Whoa!" the man exclaimed. Then in a tone of undisguised sarcasm, he added, "If you want it that badly, you can have it. Though you might try asking for it rather than simply taking it."

"Taking what?" said Rudi cautiously.

"My scarf!" the man replied.

Rudi's anger rose. "This is your scarf?"

"Whose did you think it was?" said the man.

Rudi did not answer; he simply whipped it off and tossed it to him.

The man wrapped the scarf about his throat. "You're a friendly one!"

"What can you expect when you got a gun poked in my face?" said Rudi sullenly.

The man turned the gun away from Rudi and let it rest comfortably in the crook of his arm.

"Thank you," said Rudi, rather insincerely.

"So you're Rudi," he asked. But it was not really a question.

Rudi nodded.

"I'm Oscar," the man said. And he surprised Rudi by holding out his hand.

Rudi took it grudgingly, then blurted out, "Why didn't you just come up to me? Why'd you have to come sneaking up behind me?"

"Who was sneaking up on who?" Oscar demanded.

"Well, I sure wasn't sneaking up on *you*," said Rudi. "You found me up in that tree, remember."

"That's right, looking right down on me," said Oscar. "How in the world was I to know it was you up there?"

"Because you've been following me for the past two or three hours," answered Rudi.

Oscar glanced down at him sharply. "You're out of your mind, boy," he said. "You've been in the forest too long—or not long enough, it looks like."

They both stood looking at each other suspiciously for a few moments.

"What were you doing behind me then?" Rudi asked, becoming more civil.

"I was tracking a rabbit for lunch," said Oscar, "which by the way, I've lost." Rudi could tell that he was genuinely disappointed.

"Who was following me, then?" asked Rudi.

"That's what I'm wondering," said Oscar, revealing a hint of unexpected concern.

"Maybe it was another resistance fighter, one like you."

"No, I don't think so. They'd have no reason to follow a boy. They would have either ignored you or asked you if you needed help."

"It couldn't have been a German," said Rudi. "They don't need to hide in the forest."

Oscar shot him a glance. "They're not hiding," he said. "They know we're out here. They know, and believe me, they're trying to find us. They've started sending some of their men out to comb this forest nearly every day."

"You mean it could have been a Nazi chasing me?" cried Rudi.

"Well, that's the only thing I can think of. Still, it doesn't make sense. If it had been a German, I doubt I would have found you in that tree. Unless—" He stopped and looked around cautiously. "When was the last time you heard someone following you—besides me?" he asked, turning back to Rudi.

"Well," said Rudi, "I guess it would have been a couple of hours ago. At that time, I sat down to see if whoever it was would approach me."

"You mean you just sat down and waited for this person to come after you?" Oscar said incredulously.

"I figured it was the only way," said Rudi. "I didn't want to keep looking for clues with some stranger watching, but I didn't want to get off the trail either."

"I'll say this for you," said Oscar, "you've got guts."

Rudi started to smile, but caught himself. "Don't give me too much credit. I thought it was you at first, remember. I even tied that scarf about my neck, thinking that you would recognize it."

Oscar rewarded his honesty with a cynical laugh. "I said you had guts—not brains. But that's all right. As long as you have guts, *I* can help you with the brains."

It was obvious that Rudi's crusty friend was not slow to appreciate his own talents.

"Anyway," Rudi added, "after about thirty minutes I heard whoever it was move away. I stayed an extra hour to make certain that I didn't hear any more. Then I got up and went on. I'd gone about an hour when I heard you behind me."

"And that's when you climbed a tree to see if you could catch a glimpse of me?" asked Oscar.

Rudi nodded. "Do you think maybe it was a German following me, hoping that I might lead him to you or some other soldiers?" asked Rudi.

"That's what I was thinking." Oscar gave a wry grin. "Guess you've got some brains after all."

"But why would he give up?" asked Rudi.

"Don't know."

"It's not much like a German, is it?"

"Sure isn't," Oscar agreed. "Especially not a German who's tracking someone," he added. "All I can say, boy, is you ran into one who either had lost his mind or who was struck blind when you sat down against that tree. Still, there's no guarantee that he won't be back. So we'd better get moving."

"Where exactly are we going?" asked Rudi.

"Wait and see," said Oscar.

Unwilling to take chances, Oscar not only took an indirect route but also left an intricate network of confusing tracks behind them. He doubled and redoubled his path until Rudi feared to lose sight of him.

"That German would have to be a genius to follow your trail," Rudi commented.

"Then we're safe sure enough," Oscar said.

By the time they finally reached Oscar's hideout, it was late in the afternoon. Rudi was ravenous, and he was glad when Oscar turned to him and said gruffly, "I'm starving. Never did get lunch. Think you could eat something?"

"Anything," Rudi replied.

"I think we're in luck. Although I lost one rabbit today, looks as if I've got another," he said, as he moved forward a few steps and knelt down.

Rudi went over and knelt beside him. Sure enough, there was a dead rabbit caught in one of Oscar's handmade traps.

"That's a funny-looking trap," said Rudi, observing it more closely.

A look of annoyance passed over Oscar's grim features. "Does the trick—enough to be feeding you tonight, anyway."

Rudi decided that Oscar disliked criticism almost as much as he enjoyed praise, a fact that Rudi determined to keep in mind.

"There's another good thing about this trap," Oscar continued. "It kills the game instantly, and that's important. It's cruel to use a trap that simply maims the creature and leaves it suffering for hours. Remember that," he said. Then he turned and without further comment set about the task of skinning and cleaning the rabbit.

Rudi watched with fascination as Oscar deftly did his work.

"Ready to eat?" Oscar asked when he had finally finished cleaning it.

Rudi glanced hesitantly at the carcass. "We're not going to eat him raw, are we?"

Oscar afforded himself a smile at Rudi's expense. "Only if you want to. Personally, I prefer my meat cooked."

Rudi bristled a little under Oscar's scornful gaze, but only said, "I'm with you."

"Good, that's settled," said Oscar. "Now for your first experience in cooking in a forest kitchen. First off, we want a fire that smokes as little as possible. That means we want to use dry, dead twigs. If you get them off the ground, they're usually too damp. So it's better to break them off the bushes, like this," he said, demonstrating.

Rudi followed Oscar's example, and before long they had a whole stack of twigs to work with. Oscar then took a match out of his pocket and held it up to Rudi. See that?" he said, pointing to the tip of the match. "I covered it with candle wax. Now why do you think I did that?"

Rudi shrugged.

"Think, boy! To keep them dry," said Oscar. "Matches are precious, and we can't afford to waste them."

"How do you get more when you run out?" asked Rudi.

"Villagers," said Oscar. "I make a trip to one of the farm villages nearly every night. You'd be surprised at how many people are willing to help, though it's getting more dangerous for them to do so. If the Germans catch them supplying any soldiers, they're in real trouble. Still, it's hard to stop one good Pole from helping another."

Oscar took a handful of twigs and put the match to them. Almost immediately they were aflame. "While I'm getting this fire under way, I want you to take that billy can over there, go down to the river, and fill it with water. We can boil it and have some to drink."

Rudi got the can and set off.

"Collect five or six stones on your way back too," Oscar called after him.

By the time Rudi returned with the water and stones, Oscar had cut the rabbit meat into thin, small strips and placed it on a large, flat rock. He then put the rock on the fire, and before long the meat was sizzling on this "homemade" grill.

"Want me to hold the can of water over the fire till it boils?" asked Rudi.

"Not unless you'd like to cook your fingers as well," said Oscar. "We can heat the stones you brought and drop them into the water. They'll bring it to a boil in no time, and after it's boiled awhile, it will be safe enough for us to drink."

Rudi handed him the stones he had collected.

"Now just set the can over there until I get these good and hot," Oscar said as he placed the stones on the grill beside the meat. "And hand me the rest of those twigs," he added.

Rudi turned around and started picking up the twigs for him. He had just gotten a good handful when—

BANG! BANG! BANG!

Shots rang out behind him. He spun around, expecting to find Oscar lying dead at his feet. Instead, he saw him doubled over in laughter.

"One thing's for sure," said Oscar, laughing uproariously, "if that German's anywhere close by, those explosions will probably send him running. And if they don't, the look on your face will!"

Rudi felt his temper starting to go, but he clamped down on it. He wondered if Oscar had played a trick on him just to scare him. "What in the world was that!" he asked.

"Did you get those stones from the riverbank?" Oscar asked.

"Yes, but—"

"Never heat stones that have been in the water, or even close to it, for that matter. They explode. That's why I told you to pick some up on the way back, *after* you'd gotten the water."

"Sorry."

"No harm done," Oscar said, shaking his head at Rudi's vast inexperience. "Just get me four or five more."

While collecting the stones, Rudi had time to think about the incident. When the rocks exploded, it was as if Oscar had been transformed. The fierce, wild expression had vanished, and he looked cheerful, almost comic, in appearance. Rudi would have expected most people to get angry with him for making such a blunder. But Oscar had just laughed it off. *Maybe he's not so gruff as I thought at first,* said Rudi to himself. *Maybe there's another side to him.* The thought was reassuring.

"Here's a few more," said Rudi, returning to the fire with several dry stones.

"Rabbit's almost ready," said Oscar as he turned the meat over. "I hope you like it well done."

"Suits me fine," said Rudi as he sat down close to the fire.

Oscar put the new stones on, heated them, and used them to boil the water. Once it was purified, he poured some into two small mugs made of bark. He gave one to Rudi and set the other one down for himself.

"How long has it been since you've eaten meat?" he asked as he served up the rabbit.

"Too long," Rudi replied.

"Better take your time then and chew it a good long while before swallowing," warned Oscar. "And be sure and stop eating before you're full. It'll sit hard on your stomach otherwise." Then, as though catching himself for being too soft, he added, "Last thing I want on my hands is a kid with a bellyache."

"This is great," said Rudi after taking his first bite. "It's the best thing I've tasted in months."

"I imagine it is," said Oscar. "Nature is a lot kinder to us than the Germans are."

Rudi's thoughts turned to his father, and for a moment he stopped eating. Oscar did not seem to notice.

"Out here," he continued, "you'll find that you have everything you need—not just to survive, but to survive comfortably. If you have a sharp knife, and a good head on your shoulders, you'll do fine. By the way, your father did give you a knife, didn't he?"

"Yes," said Rudi, bringing his mind back to the conversation. He pulled the knife out of his back pocket and showed it to Oscar.

"Looks good and sharp," said Oscar, taking it to examine. He then handed it back to Rudi. "Now all you have to do is learn how to use it."

"What did you use to do—before the war, I mean?" asked Rudi, returning the knife to his pocket.

"I was a teacher," said Oscar.

"What did you teach?" asked Rudi, betraying a bit of surprise, for he could not imagine this rough man standing in front of a class.

"Science and math," Oscar replied. "I used to bring my class out here to the forest several times a year. The forest is a great place to teach."

"We never got to come out here," said Rudi.

"Well, you're here now, and we'll start our classes tomorrow."

"Classes," groaned Rudi.

"Didn't think you could avoid school forever, did you? Besides, school shouldn't be a problem for a Kaplan. I know your father's a pretty smart man. You much like him?"

"I'm working on it," said Rudi.

Oscar nodded and shot a glance—almost of approval— at Rudi.

"By the way, my father said that you were part of a resistance group. I haven't seen any other soldiers. Where are the rest?" asked Rudi.

"Everywhere," said Oscar. "We break up during the day and spread out over the forest. It's safer that way. We only meet together at night."

"What do you do then?" asked Rudi.

"Anything we can to get at the Germans. You'll see tonight," he said while finishing his last bite. "When you're done there, you might want to lie down by the fire and get some rest. You won't be getting much after dark."

CHAPTER SEVENTEEN
NIGHT RAIDERS
NOV. 1939

And when ye shall hear of wars and rumours of wars,
be ye not troubled: for such things must needs be.
—Mark 13:7a

The fire had gone out. It was pitch dark and icy cold
when Oscar awakened Rudi from a deep sleep. Rudi had
never been so tired. His arms and legs felt like lead as
he unwillingly stumbled to his feet, and once standing,
he wanted so much to lie back down that it was almost
painful.

But Oscar was impatient. "We've got to get moving,"
he said, and they set out immediately.

After following the river for a few hours, they at last
emerged from the forest into a field several miles west
of the city. "Aren't you afraid someone might see us?"
Rudi asked.

"Not here," Oscar replied. "The Germans don't usually
come this far out into the country without a good reason,
especially at night."

"What if that one German's still tracking us?" asked
Rudi.

"He's not," Oscar said.

"How do you know?"

"He came back while you were sleeping," Oscar replied. "He won't be bothering us again."

"Are you sure it was the same soldier?" asked Rudi.

"I'm sure," said Oscar. "He didn't know I was there. He went straight for you."

"I wonder how he found us?"

"Well, I'd say he probably was having a pretty hard time until he heard those rocks explode," said Oscar, smiling a bit as he remembered the episode. "Most likely he was quite a bit off track until you helped him out."

"I wonder why he didn't just come after me when he caught up with me earlier?" asked Rudi.

"Me too," replied Oscar, "but it doesn't matter much now."

They continued on in silence until Rudi saw a small village in the distance.

"Is that where we're heading?" Rudi asked.

"Yes," replied Oscar.

Rudi waited for Oscar to tell him more. When he failed to continue, Rudi prodded him further. "Who are we going to see?"

"There's a widow who lives there; she's a good woman and a true patriot," he said. "Her husband was a soldier, one of those killed defending Warsaw."

"Did you know him well?"

"Yes," replied Oscar.

His tone made Rudi hesitant to ask more specific questions about the man; so he shifted the conversation back to the woman.

"Does she have any children?" he asked.

"No," said Oscar. "Just a nephew who stays with her. He's a sour-faced boy, and I don't think he likes the idea of our resistance group meeting there."

"Do you think he'd ever tell anyone about it?"

"If he dared to, I'd hate to see him after she was done with him," Oscar said. "She lets him talk, but he knows better than to try anything else."

"What should I do when we get there?"

"Sit down and enjoy the warmth of the cottage fire. And listen carefully."

Rudi and Oscar were greeted at the door by the widow. She was a tall, striking woman. Though her black hair was streaked with gray, her face had a softness that made her seem youthful and her voice a kindness that put Rudi at ease.

"You're the last to arrive," she said, addressing Oscar.

"Started a bit later than usual," he explained. "The boy needed some sleep."

"Looks as if he could have used more," she said, looking down at him. "You're Rudi?"

Rudi nodded.

"I'm Anna," she said, "and that's Josef," she added, pointing to a sullen boy sitting in the corner.

Catching Rudi's eye, Josef gave him a look of scorn that immediately put Rudi on edge. From the looks of him, Rudi guessed that Josef was three, maybe four years older than he was.

Anna led them over to the table where they joined eight men already seated.

"These are my fellow patriots," said Oscar as he and Rudi sat down.

Rudi observed the men carefully. Some of them—rough, unkempt men—looked as if they were accustomed to their tattered clothing. Others, however, seemed more like gentlemen who had not yet realized that they were dressed in rags.

Anna set a jug of *sok* (a type of fruit juice made from black currant) and some hot tea before them. She also brought a plate of meat sandwiches and wafer-thin cookies.

Rudi was suddenly wide awake, and it took all his self-control not to reach out and grab several cookies.

He looked at the others. They were talking among themselves and hardly seemed to notice that anything was set before them. It then occurred to him that none of them had that lean, hungry expression he had seen on so many faces in Warsaw.

"Hungry?" said Anna, as she set a plate and cup before him.

"He shouldn't be," said Oscar. "He had a big supper. And he probably ought not to be stuffing himself on his first day out of the city."

"Still," said Anna, "I think he can find some room for cookies."

"What do you say, Rudi?" asked Oscar with a grin. "Have any room left?"

"Plenty," said Rudi. Growing braver, he added, "Where do you get all this food? We—they're starving in Warsaw."

"The land has always been good to me," said Anna. "This year is no different, though harvest time was harder with the men off fighting." She paused and a sadness passed over her face, but it vanished the next moment.

"Such good fortune can't last forever," said Josef.

Everyone turned and looked first at Josef, then at Oscar. Although Oscar made no reply Rudi noticed that he began to pull on his mustache in irritation.

"If you're worried, why don't you join us and try doing something about it?" said one of the soldiers.

"I am doing something," Josef replied.

"And what is that?" another soldier challenged.

"I am waiting," said Josef.

"Waiting?"

"Yes! Waiting until Hitler controls Poland as he does Germany!"

In a moment one soldier was on his feet, advancing toward the boy. "You little—"

Oscar blocked his path.

"Sit down," he snapped. "He's just a stupid boy. Let him talk." The soldier sat down, and after a moment Oscar did too.

"I may be young, but I am wiser than all of you put together. It's you—you and others like you—that keep Poland in chains," Josef lashed out, heedless of the soldier's menacing look. "Once we acknowledge Hitler, he will do for us what he has done for Germany. Then there will be enough food for everyone. We have only to do as he says."

"You would sell your soul for a piece of bread!" the soldier shouted.

"And you would let thieving Jews and gypsies rob the Polish people of what is rightfully theirs."

"That's enough," warned Anna.

But Josef's comment had made Rudi so angry that he had not even heard her. "Jews aren't thieves," he said glaring at Josef.

"How would you know? You a Jew-lover? Or maybe you're a Jew yourself," said Josef, glaring back.

Oscar placed a hand on Rudi's arm, and by force of will Rudi managed to keep silent.

"He knows," said Oscar, rising from his chair and moving slowly to the corner, "because he's a bright boy, one who is smart enough *not* to listen to fools who promise bread and hand out stones."

Rudi was a little surprised at Oscar's staunch defense, but it pleased him.

Oscar stood towering over Josef, daring him to reply. Josef knew he had no chance against such an opponent. Rising from his stool, he moved out of Oscar's way. Then he left the cottage, slamming the door behind him.

"Why do you let him stay, Anna?" said one of the soldiers.

"Because he's family, and because I hope he will one day come to his senses."

"I don't know, Anna," said Oscar. "He's a bad one. Maybe you ought to make him go. He's old enough to fend for himself, and I don't see much hope of ever changing him."

She stood a moment, thinking.

"I will decide when he is past hope," she finally said to Oscar. Then turning toward the rest of the group, she added, "I will decide when it is time to make him go."

"We've wasted enough time arguing," Oscar said, returning to his seat. "Let's get to down to business. I've received word that there will be five German trucks passing about four miles from here at 3:00 in the morning."

"What are they carrying?" a soldier asked.

"Ammunition," said Oscar, smiling.

"What's the plan?" another asked.

"We take one and blow up the others."

"Why not take them all?"

"Wouldn't work. We'll have a hard enough time jumping one."

"Who's going to take the one?"

"I will," said Oscar. "I want the rest of you to spread yourselves out along the roadside, two by two, about fifty yards apart. I'll be last in line, waiting for the fifth truck to pass—that's the one I'll go for. When you see me stand up, I want you each to take aim and blow the gas tanks out of the others. If you're successful, the driver of the last truck will be so rattled, I'll have no trouble jumping the truck and overtaking him."

"And if we're not?" asked one man.

"We'll worry about that when the time comes," said Oscar.

"What about him?" said a soldier, pointing to Rudi.

"He'll be coming with us," Oscar said. Then turning to Rudi he added, "You'll hang back, however. If we fail, take to your heels as fast as you can and head straight for the woods. There will be at least enough commotion to give you time to get out of sight."

"Can you make it on your own, boy?" someone asked.

"Hopefully, he won't have to," Oscar said before Rudi could answer. "At least not until I've had a few more weeks to teach him the ropes. But if you do have to go it alone," he continued addressing Rudi, "remember, you at least know how to cook a rabbit. You needn't starve."

"Speaking of eating," Anna said, "I think you all had better finish up these sandwiches; you'll need them."

By midnight they were on their way. Rudi stayed close to Oscar. Not that he did not trust the others, but he felt that they viewed him as a burden rather than a companion.

"We've got forty minutes if they are traveling on schedule," Oscar announced when they had reached their destination. "Let's get into position now."

The men obeyed.

"I want you to move back several yards," said Oscar to Rudi as soon as the others were out of sight. "You'll be able to see what's happening—and there ought to be plenty to see—but don't stay too close. If you had any ideas about being a hero so soon, you can just forget about them. You will stay put until I come after you."

"What if you don't pull it off?" asked Rudi. "How will I know when to run for it?"

"If you see four trucks go up in flames, stay put. If fewer than that, run for it. Now go on and get settled."

While waiting, Rudi had some time to think. Up to that point he had had no chance to give thought to the consequences of the resistance groups' actions. But as he lay there in the field, he was reminded of the poster he had seen only weeks ago in the shop window. He was surprised at how many of the details he could remember. *If there is any destruction of German property . . . six people will be shot. For the death of any German soldier . . . twelve people will be shot. Five trucks, five soldiers—*

He began trying to calculate how many lives would be lost, but his thoughts were interrupted when suddenly he saw the trucks come into view.

They were moving quickly, almost as if they sensed the danger. One, two, three, four passed. Rudi saw Oscar get up. The fifth truck passed, and Oscar jumped on back of it just as the others began firing.

It seemed at first as if no one could hit his mark. Then came a deafening explosion, then another, and another. Flames leaped up as the ammunition continued to detonate, sending debris flying in every direction. The fourth truck was moving so quickly that it crashed into the third and exploded. It looked to Rudi as if the truck that carried Oscar would do the same, but within seconds of impact, it swerved off the road and into the field. Weaving madly, it continued moving at a dangerous speed until it finally overturned.

The others rushed toward the vehicle. Encircling the truck, they waited, rifles ready, while a man crawled out of the cab. Rudi could not see who it was. But when the soldiers lowered their guns, he knew that it was Oscar.

Rudi watched as they unloaded the truck and divided the ammunition among them. Each man took as much as he could carry. Then they split up, each taking a different route toward the forest.

"We did it!" said Oscar as he approached Rudi and motioned for him to get up and follow him. "That will keep them stirred up for a while, won't it?" he added as they began their march toward the woods.

It was obvious that he was waiting for some word of praise, but Rudi offered none.

"Well, thanks for the congratulations," Oscar finally said.

"I'm sorry," said Rudi. "I was just thinking about how many people will be shot for what we did tonight."

In the dim light of the forest Oscar turned to him, a silhouette of irritation. "What are you talking about?" he said.

Rudi realized that Oscar had no idea of the lists that were posted in the city. He explained.

"Well, what are we supposed to do?" he said when Rudi finished telling him. "Are we just supposed to stand by and let them have their way?"

Rudi said nothing. Oscar stopped and took him by the shoulder.

"Listen, boy, do you think that they would stop shooting people if we stopped fighting back?" he asked. "The Jews don't do anything to the Nazis, and the Nazis still shoot them down in the streets or round them up for the work camps."

The words went home to Rudi, and he remembered his father standing in the truck as they took him away. "I'm not saying we should stop fighting," he said quietly.

"Well, then what are you saying?" Oscar demanded.

"Only that I wish there were some other way to win," said Rudi.

Oscar stood looking down at Rudi for a moment more, then slowly turned. He kept his hand on Rudi's shoulder and led him back into the forest.

CHAPTER EIGHTEEN
ANOTHER GOOD-BYE
DEC. 1939

A word fitly spoken is like apples of gold in pictures of silver.

—Proverbs 25:11

"Your life depends on your ability to observe the world around you," said Oscar the next morning when he and Rudi started out for Rudi's first full lesson in survival. "From what I can tell," Oscar continued, sharpening his knife on a rough stone as they walked along, "you haven't seen or heard anything since you entered the woods."

Rudi was growing a little tired of Oscar's comments on his inexperience in the forest. "I haven't been as bad as all that," he retorted.

"No?" asked Oscar. He stopped abruptly. "Close your eyes," he said defiantly.

"What for?"

"Just do as I say."

Rudi obeyed.

"Now, tell me what kind of tree you're standing beside."

"I don't know the name of it," answered Rudi.

"Then just describe it," said Oscar.

Rudi hesitated. "It looks like any other tree," he finally said in exasperation.

"Like any other tree," his tutor mocked. "Do you know how many kinds of trees there are in the world, boy? And you're going to stand there and tell me they all look alike?"

"Well, I didn't say *that,* exactly," said Rudi, opening his eyes.

"Keep those eyes closed," Oscar ordered, "and hold out your hand."

As Rudi stretched out his hand, he felt Oscar lay something in his palm.

"There, I've given you a clue," Oscar said. "Now tell me what kind of tree it is."

Rudi ran his fingers over a tiny branch.

"Its a tree with needles, not leaves," he said, fearing to be any more specific.

"Well," said Oscar, "at least you didn't tell me it was a Christmas tree. But feel it carefully. Are the needles short or long?"

"Long—I think," said Rudi. "They feel kind of droopy," he added.

"Okay. Are they pointed or blunt at the tip?"

"Pointed," said Rudi.

"Since you're so observant, open your eyes and look at the branch closely."

Rudi did so.

"That's a branch from a Douglas fir tree," Oscar told him. "If it had been a black spruce, the needles would have been short. If it had been a red cedar, they would have been small and scale-like. There are all kinds of needle trees. By the way," he added, "now that you know the name of at least one tree, look around again. Are all the trees about you Douglas fir trees?"

"No," said Rudi sheepishly.

"Well, your first lesson's complete. You've learned how little you know." Oscar gave his usual smirk, but then he added, more earnestly, "Now I'll be able to teach you how to really see, hear, feel, and even taste and smell like you never have before."

Oscar was true to his word. Under his instruction, Rudi experienced a whole new world opening before him, and as he entered into it, he felt himself growing in body and mind. His improved forest diet made him physically stronger, and Oscar's merciless drilling forced him to be mentally alert.

His senses became so acute that before long he could identify many of the trees and bushes not just by sight but by touch. He could discern by taste or smell whether nuts and berries were safe to eat, and he could hear even the smallest creatures scrambling through a thicket.

He also became skillful in adapting and improvising. He learned not one but several ways to trap, prepare, and cook meat. And he was careful, as Oscar had instructed him, to include the fat parts of the rabbit in his diet. He also learned how to build lean-to's, construct bush ladders, and even how to weave a rope from reeds collected from the river bank.

The visits to Anna's farm were his contact with the outside world. Except for Josef, the men were friendly. Occasionally he accompanied them on their "missions," but Oscar seldom allowed Rudi to participate, saying in his gruff way that he did not want any boy getting himself shot. Rudi was grateful, for he had a feeling that Oscar was really trying to protect him. Most often, the men went out without him, and he met Oscar later at a rendezvous point deep in the forest.

By late December, Rudi was proud of how independent he had grown. Although Oscar never came right out and said so, Rudi felt sure that he was proud of him as well.

"You've learned a lot over the past few weeks," Oscar admitted as he and Rudi set out for their usual nightly meeting at Anna's. "But I still have a few more tricks up my sleeve."

Rudi was curious. "Like what?"

"Well, now," Oscar said, and he afforded himself and Rudi a genuine smile, "if I told you, then I'd be talking myself out of a job."

"Aw, you don't have anything," said Rudi.

"Maybe, maybe not," said Oscar.

As they approached Anna's, they saw that the straw roof to the underground cooler was propped open. Oscar headed for it.

"Anna?" he called.

"Yes?" she answered.

"Just making sure no one was stealing your food," said Oscar, peering down at her. "Rudi would be glad to help you carry anything in if you need it."

"I can manage," she replied. "You two go on in. I think the men have some news for you."

When they entered, Rudi noticed that there did not seem to be the usual hubbub going on. Several of the men were conversing in low tones while Josef moved about the table, trying to overhear what they were saying.

"What's the news?" asked Oscar, settling himself down in his usual place at the head of the table.

The men seemed to hesitate. Their secretive manner was unusual.

"Come on," Oscar snapped. "Out with it. We haven't got all night."

"Not with him in the room," said one of the rough-looking soldiers, gesturing toward Josef.

"You've never minded my being here before," said Josef.

"I mind it now," the soldier replied.

Josef pointed at Rudi. "You let *him* stay."

"That's because he doesn't make speeches about how Hitler is going to save Poland."

"Don't worry," said Josef. "I've given up making speeches to your kind."

"And I've given up making speeches *in front of* your kind," replied the soldier.

A heated argument seemed inevitable, but just then Anna entered. She was carrying a large sack of potatoes. The men quieted, but she had heard enough to know that trouble was brewing.

"Go out and gather some kindling," she said to her nephew.

"That can wait," said Josef.

"No," she said, walking over to him. "It can't." And the look in her eye discouraged him from further argument.

Reluctantly he put on his hat and coat and went out to get more wood.

As soon as Josef had closed the door behind himself, Anna approached the table and laid the sack down. She began collecting bread and cheese for them as well.

"What's all this?" asked Oscar, growing annoyed at their secrecy.

"I asked her if she had any food she could spare," replied the man who had just been arguing with Josef. "We'll be needing it for our trip."

Oscar, impatient at the best of times, glared at the soldier. "What trip?" he shouted. "Will you get to the point!"

"We're planning to move closer to the Germans' stronghold," the soldier said.

"I've gotten word from a reliable source on the location of a major German supply line," a second soldier announced, somewhat boastfully.

"With the ammunition we have been able to get, we could do some real damage," another explained.

Rudi had never seen the men so animated. They spoke excitedly, cutting in one upon another.

"By blocking off their food and ammunition, we could weaken their whole front line."

"These skirmishes we've been involved in are barely noticeable."

"This is our chance to do more."

"But we have to move quickly. The Germans are constantly shifting the supply line for protection."

"Hold on, here," Oscar demanded.

Everyone grew quiet.

"How far away is this?" he asked.

"It would take us about two days to get there," said the rough-looking man.

Oscar sat thinking a moment, running his fingers over his beard. Then he turned to Rudi. "What do you think? Do you want to go?"

"How long would we be gone?" asked Rudi.

"We don't plan on coming back until this war's won," said one soldier with a thump of his rifle butt on the floor.

"If we succeed on this expedition," another explained, "we move farther up the line."

Rudi hesitated. The thought of moving farther from Warsaw was not at all appealing. Still, he did not want to lose Oscar, either.

"I don't think I'd be much help," he said. Then he added, more out of duty than conviction, "But I don't see why you can't go, Oscar."

"I'm not leaving you," Oscar replied.

Rudi glanced up, relieved and a little pleased to hear him say so. Embarrassed, Oscar scowled at his men as though he had not said anything at all.

"Listen, Oscar, we need you," one of his men pleaded.

"Besides, for weeks now you've been bragging about how smart the boy is," someone added.

Rudi looked at Oscar and noticed that he was fidgeting in his chair. This time the gruff man could not ignore what had been said.

"Well, I have told them that you're doing pretty well," Oscar admitted. "Of course, they know it's because you've had a good teacher."

"That's right. He's had a good teacher. Now he can make it on his own. You can, can't you?" asked the rough-looking man, turning toward Rudi.

"Yeah, I guess so," Rudi said unenthusiastically.

"Why don't you want to go?" Oscar asked him.

"When my father comes back," he said, "he'll come back to Warsaw. I want to be close by when he does."

The men at the table said nothing, but several of them exchanged glances, and Rudi could see by their expressions that they did not think his father would ever really return.

Rudi was trying hard not to let their skepticism overtake him, but he seemed to be losing the battle until Anna interrupted.

"The boy's right," she said. "When his father returns, he will come first to Warsaw looking for him."

"You think he should stay?" asked Oscar, turning to her.

"I do," she said.

Rudi felt hopeful once again.

"Then you should stay," Oscar concluded, turning back to Rudi. Then he added after some hesitation, "But I must go with the others."

Rudi tried to hide his disappointment but could not.

"I must go," Oscar continued, "because I want to do my part to end this war. I want to make sure that men like your father can return as soon as possible."

Rudi nodded but still said nothing.

Oscar turned to his men. "When do we leave?"

"Tonight," the first soldier said.

"That way we can make the attack on Christmas Eve," another explained. "They'll be sure to be doing some celebrating. Their guard will be down."

Oscar looked doubtful. "Are we ready?"

"Yes," the men replied in unison.

"A couple of us met earlier this afternoon to collect the ammunition we had hidden," the rough-looking man told him. "And, of course, Anna has provided these supplies."

"Then I guess that settles it," said Oscar.

He placed a hand on Rudi's shoulder before getting up to leave.

"Here, take this," he said, and he unwrapped his red woolen scarf from about his neck and handed it to Rudi. "You'll need it more than I will. Besides, I can get it from you when I return," he said, and then he turned to go.

Rudi took the scarf and lingered behind, waiting for the remaining soldiers to take their leave.

"You're welcome to stay here until Oscar returns, Rudi," said Anna, approaching him as he stood in the doorway of the cottage.

He was about to take her offer when he saw Josef returning. Remembering Josef's bitter speeches, Rudi decided to go back to the forest. There was no denying the fact that, if he stayed with Anna, Josef would provoke him. A fight would be inevitable—and unwise.

"Thanks, but I'll make it just fine," he said. "Oscar's been a great teacher. Just ask him—he'll tell you so himself."

"I have no doubt that you'll make it," she said. "But remember," she continued, as if she sensed what he was thinking, "you need never be afraid to come here. I'll be here if you ever do need anything—anything," and, bending down, she kissed him on the cheek.

Her words gave Rudi both courage and comfort. "I'll remember," he said. And as he turned to go, he determined that when the war was over, he was going to bring her the biggest, brightest bouquet of flowers he could find.

CHAPTER NINETEEN
CHRISTMAS MEMORIES
DEC. 1939

*For a man's life consisteth not in the abundance of the
things which he possesseth.*

—Luke 12:15b

Several long, cold days had passed. It was Christmas
Eve. Rudi sat alone in the forest by the fire, warming
himself and thinking on all the Christmases that had gone
before.

He saw himself beside a different fire, his father seated
next to him. They had had their fill of Christmas dinner,
and were now settling down to read the Christmas story
and open their presents. Rudi recalled his father's strong,
mellow voice as he read the Scripture. He then remembered
the look of pleasure on his father's face as he watched
Rudi examine each new gift he opened. He remembered,
too, his own feeling of satisfaction when he saw that his
father was pleased with the gift Rudi had carefully chosen
for him.

Such memories tumbled into Rudi's mind one upon
another. As they did, he began to realize something about
all the Christmas Eves and mornings he had known. He
began to awaken to the fact that all the pleasant memories

were not centered in the warmth of fires, in the food or festivities, or even in the presents. They were centered in his father.

Even in the forest he could make a fire. And thanks to Oscar, he could also find a way to eat his fill. As for the presents, Rudi was certain that even if he had had a cartload of gifts, they could not have cheered him.

"People, people are important, Rudi, not things." How many times he had heard his father say those words, but only now did he feel that he truly understood.

Reaching inside his coat pocket, he pulled out his mother's last unopened letter. He ran his fingers over it carefully. Despite his care, it had become wrinkled and soiled during his traveling in the forest.

Perhaps, he thought, *I'll go ahead and open it tonight.* He reasoned that his birthday seemed so very far away, and reading the letter now would be something special he could do, something that would make the night seem more like Christmas Eve.

He laid the envelope across his knee and gently ran his hands over it to smooth it out. Then with a decisive air he turned it over and tore it open, and leaning close to the fire, he unfolded it and began to read.

for Nov. 15, 1940

Dear Rudi,

In my first letter I promised you that in later letters I would tell you more of what I knew about your father. Since this is probably the last letter I will be writing you, it is time to keep that promise.

I'll begin by telling you that I have known few men who are as strong, as wise, or as kind as your father. He possesses qualities that evoke respect from men in any age. Had he lived in another time, he might have been a gallant knight, a noble warrior, or a worthy sage.

Of course, there would be those who would discredit my account of him by saying that I see him too much through love's eyes. But I am safe with you, for I imagine that you see him through the same eyes. And to such critics we can say, who would know him better than you and I? I would point out, too, that if a man can earn the love and admiration of his family, he will have little difficulty in securing the respect of his neighbors. Any honest man admits that it is easier to be thought noble in public than it is to be consistently so at home.

But enough of "public" opinion. My concern is not with your father's reputation, for I think we both agree on the kind of man he is. My concern is that you know how he came to be such a man. It can be stated simply: He learned early the importance of dying to self. And I have watched him die again and again over the years. If you will watch him closely, you will see the same. Don't misunderstand me: it has not always been easy for him. Dying is never easy. Despite the hardship, however, he has seldom failed.

But how can a man—or boy—know that he has succeeded in dying to self? You must ask yourself: Can I easily forgive someone who's hurt me? Can I cheerfully meet someone else's need, knowing that I will never receive anything in return? Or can I do some good deed or accomplish some hard task and be content that another receives the credit for what I have done?

If you can do such things, Rudi, you have begun to die to self. For you have ceased rejoicing in the glory that doing good can bring and have started rejoicing in the good itself.

So, I ask you, son, while you are young, to die willingly. Until you do, you will be only a shadow of what you could become. As you know, a shadow only looks like a man. Long ago your father ceased being a shadow and became a man. Be as he is, Rudi, and neither God nor I shall ever have cause to be disappointed in you.

Love,

Mother

As Rudi sat by the fire and thought about his mother and father, he was filled with a longing unlike any he had ever known. It was a longing for the world to be as God intended it, and with the longing came a desire that he should help to make it so.

It seemed for the first time that he had begun to see things clearly. Having seen, he felt that he could never again be satisfied with the heroic deeds that took place only in his imagination.

Lost in such thought, Rudi failed to feed the fire, and he now realized that it was dwindling. A winter sleet had started. Rather than try to rekindle the fire, he decided that it would be better for him to head toward one of the villages and find an open barn to sleep in. There he could stay dry and get a good night's sleep as well. Besides, he felt like walking. After throwing snow on the last embers of the fire, he set out.

At dawn the next morning Rudi was half-roused from sleep by a rustling sound. It was faint, so faint that he soon decided he had been only dreaming. He turned on his side, and the strong smell of damp hay reminded him that he was inside someone's barn and that he needed to get up and move on before the day began. Reluctantly he stood, brushed himself off, and headed toward the ladder at the end of the loft. He had just started his descent when he heard the rustling sound again. He had not been dreaming. He scanned the loft carefully, but it was still very early and difficult to see clearly. He thought of climbing back up and taking a closer look but decided against it. It seemed wiser to get moving.

He made his descent as quickly as possible and headed for the door. But as he did, he turned back and thought he saw the outline of another figure coming down the ladder. He would have bolted out the door, but the form seemed small and unsteady.

Deciding he had nothing to fear, he returned to the foot of the ladder and waited. It wasn't long before a little girl stepped down and stood before him. As she stood looking up at him expectantly, he noticed that she held a ragged stuffed rabbit tightly by the ear.

It occurred to him that he had possibly been sleeping in her family's barn. But he quickly dismissed the thought, for he could not imagine any parents sending their little girl out to sleep in the loft.

He then remembered Oscar telling him of children who slept in barns and begged food from the villagers. But surely this little girl was too young to succeed at such a life. By her size, he guessed that she could be no more than about three or four.

"What are you doing here?" he asked.

She said nothing. She simply stood there as if waiting for Rudi to do something.

He knelt down to get a better look at her. It was then he realized that he had seen this little girl before. It was the same little girl that he had cared for his first day at the hospital . . . the same one whose sister had been killed in the field.

Although she was paler, thinner than she had been before, she was still a lovely little girl. Her dark hair and large, dark eyes made her skin by contrast seem that much whiter.

Rudi and his father had been forced to leave the hospital before she recovered from her wounds. As a result they had never discovered whether her mother and father had been found. Now he hesitated to ask.

"Where do you live?" he finally asked.

She still said nothing. And he remembered his father's saying, "She has not said a word since one of the soldiers brought her here."

It occurred to him that maybe she never had said anything, or at least had not spoken since that first day he had met her. He wondered if she even understood what he was saying, and he decided to try one more time.

"Do you sleep here every night?" he asked.

It was no use; she would not or could not reply.

"Well," he said, standing, "you're welcome to come along with me—that is, if you don't have anywhere else to go. I can take care of you. I can get us things to eat and make sure that we are warm and dry at night."

A faint smile spread across her face.

"Come on, if you want," he said, moving toward the door. "We really should get out of here before the farmers wake up. You know they wake up awfully early."

Catching up to him, she reached up and took his hand. It seemed so small inside his own.

"You know," he said, stopping, "I don't even know your name, and since you don't seem to be able to tell me, I'm going to have to think of something to call you. I mean, I can't go around calling you 'little girl,' can I?"

He waited, but she made no gesture or change of expression to indicate whether she objected.

"How about if I call you Ingrid? That was my mother's name, and it's a very pretty name, I think. Is that all right with you?"

She nodded. Rudi was encouraged. Despite her silence she definitely understood what was said to her.

"Good," he said. "Then it's settled."

He pushed the barn door open carefully and looked out. Everything was still quiet. He stepped out, keeping a firm hold on her hand.

They had gotten past the farmer's cottage and were heading toward the open field, when the little girl stopped abruptly.

"What's wrong?" asked Rudi. She had suddenly become frightened.

"Come on," he urged. "We really must be going; there's not much time."

Still she would not move.

He looked out over the field trying to see if there was anything to frighten her. There was nothing.

The field, he thought, looking down at her. *Maybe it's the field that she's afraid of. After all, how can she be sure that there are not German planes waiting for her to step out into the open space again?*

Still, they had to cross that field. There was no other way into the forest.

"How about if I carry you?" he said, testing her.

She remained immovable, looking down at the ground before her.

"I promise that I won't let anything happen," he assured her.

She looked up slowly and studied his face for several moments. At last she reached up and let him take her, and as he set out across the field, he remembered: it was Christmas morning.

CHAPTER TWENTY
A CHRISTMAS TREASURE
DEC. 1939

*The liberal soul shall be made fat: and he that watereth
shall be watered also himself.*
—Proverbs 11:25

"How about walking now?" suggested Rudi as soon
as they reached the edge of the woods.

Ingrid was willing, so Rudi set her down and took
her by the hand.

"We have to stay deep in the forest during the daylight,"
he said as he led her along. "It isn't safe otherwise. You
see, the Germans send their soldiers out here nearly every
day to look for people like us. Oscar told me that. Oscar's
a friend of mine, the man my father had me meet the
first day I got out of Warsaw."

Rudi had not had anyone to talk to for several days,
and he was thoroughly enjoying himself, even though he
was having to do all the talking.

"It's been getting worse for the villagers too," he
continued. "I heard that the Nazis have been visiting the
farmers the last few days and threatening them. Boy, that
would really make Oscar mad if he were here. You see,
Oscar and I have this friend in one of the villages. Her

name's Anna. She said I could stay with her if I wanted, but I decided to stay out here instead. And now with things getting more dangerous, I'm even afraid to go and visit her. She has this nephew—"

Rudi stopped, for at that moment he looked down at Ingrid. Her expression suddenly made him realize that his conversation was not very comforting to her.

"You don't have to worry, though," he added, trying to sound more encouraging. "I can take care of you." She didn't look as if she had been convinced. He tried again.

"Really, Ingrid, everything will be fine. Oscar taught me not only how to live out here but also how to outsmart the Germans."

She began to look somewhat relieved.

"And maybe a little later, it'll be all right to go and see Anna," he added cheerfully. "You'd like Anna. She's good at outsmarting Germans too."

When at last Ingrid seemed satisfied, Rudi determined that it might be best for him to keep quiet for a while.

They had traveled in silence for more than an hour when Ingrid suddenly let go of Rudi's hand and sat down on a nearby stump.

"Come on, Ingrid," he urged. "We haven't gone far enough yet."

But instead of getting up again, she drew her legs up close to her body, tucked her rabbit securely in her lap and put her head down on her knees.

Her reaction irritated Rudi until he noticed that her bare legs were scratched and bleeding, and the shoes she had on were so worn that they scarcely protected her feet from the winter cold. Until that moment, he had not given the slightest thought to how ill-prepared she was for such travel.

"Why didn't you tell me you were getting all scratched up?" said Rudi, sitting down beside her.

But he had no sooner gotten the question out of his mouth than he realized how stupid it sounded. By sitting down, she was trying to tell him.

"We still have a way to go, but I can carry you on my back," he suggested.

She turned her face toward him.

"You won't get too heavy that way," he said.

After a moment more, she stood up. Clutching her rabbit firmly by the ear, she waited for Rudi to hoist her up.

As they continued, Rudi stopped to check several traps he had set along the way. There were seven in all, and they were just coming up on the third.

"We've got one," said Rudi as he let Ingrid slide down off his back onto the ground.

Releasing the animal from the trap, he held it up proudly. "Look," he said, expecting at least a smile from her.

But Ingrid was not impressed. Obviously she preferred living, or at least stuffed, rabbits to dead ones.

Now I know what Oscar must have felt like the night he wanted me to compliment him for exploding all those trucks, Rudi said to himself, as he let the hand which held the rabbit drop to his side.

"I wouldn't have killed it if we didn't need it," he said. "But we have to eat, and this will taste really good. A lot better than what you've been eating, I bet. You'll see."

He set the rabbit on the ground and knelt down to let Ingrid get on his back again. Once he had gotten her comfortably settled, he picked up his game and moved on.

"If I can catch another one of these," he said, looking down at her worn shoes, "I'll make you a Christmas present."

As he had hoped, another trap yielded him a second rabbit.

It was noon before Rudi was satisfied with their location. He set Ingrid down and immediately cleared a space about six feet in circumference.

"That tree will be good for helping us build a fire that'll keep us warm right through the night," he said, pointing to a dead tree that had fallen close to the edge of his clearing. "That can be our main burning log. Now what we need are some twigs to start it up and some kindling to keep it going. Why don't you collect the twigs? Just make sure they're dry, like this one," he said, showing her. "While you're doing that, I can get the heavier sticks we'll need to keep the fire fed."

Ingrid was delighted to help and very proud of herself when she returned to Rudi with a small fistful of matted wet leaves mixed up with a few twigs.

"Uh, that's great," he said. "Maybe you could find a few more?"

She dropped what she had at his feet. While she was off looking for more, Rudi quickly set out to replace what she had brought him. And by the time she returned with her second handful, he had all the dry twigs he needed.

"Thanks, Ingrid, I think we're just about ready," he said, taking out his knife. "All I need to do now is just break these thick sticks up a bit. By carving small notches opposite each other every so often like this," he said showing her as he did so, "I can break them over my knee real easy."

Rudi soon had the fire ablaze and Ingrid seated comfortably on a log beside it. He then set out to pitch a lean-to to shelter them for the night. Most of the time he was able to get one up in less than an hour, for he always saved his lashings, and there were usually several thick branches lying about the forest floor. All he had to do was collect eight or ten of them, tie them together, prop them up, and cover them with pine branches.

To keep them even warmer, he built the shelter with the open side toward the fire. He also lashed several shorter branches together to form a small barrier. This he placed on the other side of the fire to reflect the heat into the lean-to.

As he worked, he also watched Ingrid. Remembering how fascinated he had been the first time he watched Oscar set up for the night, he said, "If you stick with me, I'll teach you a lot of new things." His comment pleased her.

Once the lean-to was finished, he skinned and cleaned the rabbits they had caught. Then after cutting the meat into small strips and laying it on his stone grill, he turned to Ingrid. "You stay here and watch the meat. I'm going right over there a way and start a smaller fire for something else. I'll be back before the thc meat's done."

After their morning travel, she was more than content to sit and enjoy the warmth of the fire and watch the meat sizzle on the grill.

Rudi made his way just out past the clearing. He was still close enough, however, to keep an eye on Ingrid. He built a small fire, making sure the flame was low, for this one was not for warmth. Once he had gotten it started, he crisscrossed several logs to surround it. He then collected some damp leaves and placed them in the spaces between the logs. After a few minutes, when the leaves were warm and dry, he put them carefully in his pocket. Next he set up eight tall sticks about the fire and draped the rabbit skins over the sticks to dry out.

"Looks like it's almost time to eat," he said, returning to Ingrid and turning the meat over on the grill. "But while we're waiting for that to finish, I want to show you something that will help keep your feet from getting cold even when we don't have a fire going."

Removing the leaves from his pocket, he knelt down beside her and took her shoes and socks off. He then wrapped leaves around her feet and put her socks back on.

"Those leaves will keep your feet insulated—you know, warm."

She looked down and tried wiggling her toes. She then began to frown, and Rudi started worrying.

"It really helps, Ingrid," he said. "Look, I put leaves in my boots, too."

Once he had shown her the leaves in his own socks, she held her feet up for him to put her shoes back on. He had won.

As Rudi dished up Ingrid's dinner, he was careful to give her all the warnings Oscar had given him his first day in the forest. He soon discovered, however, that she did not need to be told to eat slowly or lightly. Food did not seem to interest her as it did him. By the time he had finished his third helping, she was still dawdling with her first.

"I'm going over to check my other fire," he said. "And I want you to finish that by the time I get back. I didn't give you very much. But it's really important that you eat. It helps you keep warm in this cold and keeps you from getting sick. I wouldn't know what to do if you got sick, you know." But the warning seemed to have little effect until he added, "I'll give you your Christmas present as soon as you're done." When he got up to leave, she was eating.

The rabbit skins were not dry yet. He returned to the lean-to and worked on it some more, tidied the camp, and sat by the fire while Ingrid picked at her food. He checked on the skins again. They were almost ready.

Since he still had some time, Rudi sat down and picked up a rough stone to sharpen his knife while he waited. After about fifteen minutes more, he removed the skins

from the props and worked them hard over a fallen branch as though he were buffing a shoe or boot with them. Then taking his knife, he cut each skin into a large square. And putting the fire out, he returned to Ingrid.

"Come on over here," he said to Ingrid as he laid one of the two squares flat on the ground. "Now take off your shoe, and put your foot right in the middle of that square."

As she did so, Rudi folded the rabbit skin over her toes and gathered it up around the sides and heel of her foot. He then tied it around her ankle with one of his extra lashings. To his surprise, she had her other shoe off before he could even get the second piece of fur laid out.

"Now you have some soft, warm shoes just like mine," he said as he tied on her other boot. "And as soon as I can catch another rabbit," he added, "I'll make you a pair of mittens to match."

When Rudi finally looked up at Ingrid, the smile on her face reminded him of the Christmases that he had known before. Her happiness did much to help lighten the darkness of the winter forest and to take away the sadness of that Christmas day.

CHAPTER TWENTY-ONE
A NARROW ESCAPE
JAN. 1940

He sent from above, he took me, he drew me out of many waters. He delivered me from my strong enemy, and from them which hated me: for they were too strong for me.

—Psalm 18:16-17

Rudi stopped and looked about him. A heavy snow was beginning to fall, and the morning seemed especially gray. The cold of the previous night had forced him and Ingrid to seek the shelter of a barn. Now they were heading back to the forest. Rudi glanced down at Ingrid, who was shivering almost uncontrollably. Should he risk stopping to build a fire? Or should he wait until they reached a safer place? As he stood there thinking, he listened to the trees creak and groan under the weight of the ice that had formed on their limbs. It was definitely cold. He stopped.

It was difficult getting a fire started under such conditions, but over the past weeks Rudi had become a master at building fires. Before long he managed to create a tiny flame which he fed and nurtured until the small clearing was ablaze with light and warmth.

He sat Ingrid on his lap and drew himself as close to the fire as he dared. Ingrid soon stopped her shivering and grew drowsy. Resting her head against his shoulder, she fell asleep.

We should get moving again, Rudi reasoned to himself. But Ingrid's contentment and the warm tingling sensation in his hands and feet discouraged him from obeying his reason, and he yielded to his desire to stay by the fire.

Within the hour, however, he regretted his decision, for in the distance he heard dogs barking. Though the sound was still very faint, it was clear enough to rouse his fears and force him into immediate action.

"Come on, Ingrid," he said, standing her on her feet. "Help me get some snow on this fire." She was still in a sleepy stupor, but she obeyed as best she could. His mind raced as he threw leaves and branches about the clearing they had made. *You must cover your tracks carefully,* he thought. *You've already made one mistake; you can't afford another. I know I can outwit the soldiers. But the dogs—how can I fool the dogs?*

"That's enough," he said, turning to Ingrid. He then knelt down so that he could look directly at her. "You've got to listen carefully," he told her. "We may be in a little trouble, but if you do exactly as I say, things'll be all right. Do you understand?"

She nodded.

"Good. Now climb up on my back and hang on," he instructed her.

He moved quickly, backtracking periodically in an effort to make his trail confusing. But he soon realized that backtracking was costing him valuable time. The Germans and their dogs were gaining on them. Giving up the idea of disguising his trail, he headed straight for the nearest river. He knew it was frozen, but he had an idea.

Once he had reached its bank, he traveled on until the river narrowed to a width of about eight feet. The ice was fairly new, formed during the previous day and night's hard freeze and not yet covered by snow.

"Hang on as tight as you can," he said to Ingrid as soon as he had stopped. "I've got to use my hands, but I don't want to let you get down."

She clung to him so tightly that she nearly choked him, but he did not complain. He knew that it was better to bear the strain of Ingrid's weight than to let her down and risk having the dogs pick up her scent. The fact that they could pick up his was bad enough.

Scanning the area, he found two good-sized branches, dragged them over to the river's edge, and eventually managed to form a bridge across the river. He stood a few seconds to catch his breath. "I'm going to take you over to the other side," he then said. "But you're going to have to be as still as possible. If I lose my balance, we'll both end up falling through the ice." He shifted her weight to the most comfortable position and then stepped out onto the logs. His legs trembled. As he stood trying to steady himself, he heard the dogs again. Their sound convinced him that they had caught the scent and were now on his trail.

Starting out, he slid his right foot forward too far and began to topple. Quickly he drew his left foot up parallel to his right and waited until he was again steady. Then he moved his right foot forward, this time only slightly. Thus, inch by inch, he made his way across the logs.

"All right, Ingrid," he said, jumping onto the opposite side. "Hang on tight again; I've got to get up that tree."

It took all the strength he had to hoist them both up into the tree. But spurred on by fear, he managed to continue climbing.

"Now, you sit up here, and I'll be back," he said as he settled her on a high branch. There was a look of terror in her eyes as he began his descent. "Don't look down," he said. "Just sit still. I'll be back up in a minute."

He was sliding down from limb to limb so fast that his hands and face were getting terribly scratched from the bark. But he had no time to worry about such things. As soon as he reached the ground, he ran back to the riverbank and began recrossing the bridge. This time he crawled on his hands and knees, enabling him to make it in less than half the time.

Once on the other side, he took up a heavy stick. He intended to use it to break through the ice and make his pursuers think that he had fallen through.

Lifting the heavy stick over his head, he brought it down with all his might onto the ice. It cracked. Again he raised it and struck a blow. He had broken through. But as he looked at his work, he knew that it was not good enough. The cracks that extended from the hole were not long enough or numerous enough. In order to convince them, he would have to actually use his weight to break through.

By this time, Rudi could hear that the dogs were in a frenzy. They knew they were close. So did he. Quickly, he sat down and removed his boots and socks. He then took off his shirt and coat. Tying everything up in his coat, he tossed the bundle over to the other side of the bank. He then stepped out onto the ice. It held firm. He squatted down, then jumped up and came back down with a crash. The icy water that covered him was so cold that he was momentarily paralyzed. He felt as if he were drowning. Then his feet found the bottom of the river, and he stood. His head was above the water. *Move! Get out, you idiot!* he yelled at himself. But the cold reached out and seemed to hold each joint and muscle in a viselike grip. To move was agony. *Help me, Lord,* he prayed, and he soon found enough strength to grab hold of one of the logs and pull himself out of the water and onto his makeshift bridge.

He lay balanced across the logs, panting until he began to hear not only dogs but also voices. He struggled to his hands and knees and recrossed the river.

As soon as he reached the bank, he slid on his boots, put on his coat, and hurriedly stuffed the rest of his clothing down inside his coat. Then standing near the hole, he lifted the first log by its end. Carefully walking atop the second log, he half dragged, half carried the first one into the brush. From the riverbank he hauled up the second log and dragged it away. A fallen branch, covered with leaves and snow, lay across a thicket. He pulled it out and used it to try and cover the tracks made by the logs and his feet on the snowy riverbank. Summoning his last vestige of strength, he made it up the tree. Snow plopped off its branches and fell below, covering up more of the tracks. A trained woodsman like Oscar would have read the clumps of fallen snow as a sure sign that someone was up the tree, but Rudi guessed that the soldiers were not that experienced.

"Here! Over here," Rudi heard one of the soldiers shout. "Looks like whoever it was fell through."

The dogs quieted once they reached the river, for the scent had stopped at the hole in the ice.

"How deep's the river?" Rudi heard the second soldier ask.

"I don't know," the first one said. "But I'm sure it's deep enough to drown a man."

"Maybe," said the other.

The uncertainty in the second soldier's voice made Rudi anxious, for already his trousers were stiff and frozen, and his hands and feet had almost lost all sense of feeling. He had to get to a fire soon, or he would freeze to death.

"Even if it wasn't all that deep," the first soldier reasoned, "if anyone fell through, he'd drown. The cold would freeze him stiff before he could ever work up enough strength to pull himself out."

Rudi heard rustling, and moments later the second soldier said, "Here, shove this stick down there, and see how deep it is."

Rudi heard a splash.

"At least five feet," the first answered. "Once someone fell in, I assure you he wouldn't be able to get out." Then after a prolonged silence, he added, "Besides, even if he did, he'd freeze to death out here once he'd gotten wet. Come on. Otherwise, we'll be frozen too."

"I suppose you're right," the second soldier finally agreed. "I am getting hungry. Let's get going."

The first man seemed enthusiastic about that. "Good idea! There will be plenty of time after lunch to chase resistance fighters and runaway Jews."

Thank you, Lord, Rudi murmured as he listened to the soldiers' laughter fade away.

Then as he and Ingrid climbed down from their hiding place, he prayed, *Now just keep them away long enough for me to get a fire going that will dry my trousers and get the blood moving in my veins again.*

By this time, Rudi wondered if he would even be able to build a fire. As he began gathering kindling, he realized that there was no feeling left in his hands. Though he could see himself pick up the twigs, he could not feel his hands clutching them.

"Here, Ingrid," he said, "hold on to these twigs for me a couple of seconds."

He vigorously beat his hands against his thighs in an effort to get his circulation going again. It worked, and soon he began to feel a prickling sensation in his fingers. Ingrid seemed a bit frightened by his strange behavior.

"It's all right, Ingrid," he assured her. "I'm just so cold I can hardly hold on to anything. So we've got to work fast."

He was finally able to complete the foundation for the fire. Then came the most difficult part—lighting the match. He had never felt so clumsy. After again slapping his hands against his thighs for a few moments, he drew a match out of his pocket and tried to strike it. It took several times before he was successful, but at last the fire blazed.

He built the fire close to the trunk of an enormous tree that had fallen. It reflected the heat a little bit, making a nice warm space between itself and the flames. He sat on top of the trunk, hands stretched out, wet trousers as close to the flames as he could get without singeing them. He glanced at Ingrid. "We're going to have to stay here about an hour until I'm good and thawed out."

Reluctantly, she came and sat down beside him.

"It'll be all right. They've gone," he said. "And God will keep them away," he added emphatically.

His words seemed to satisfy her and at the same time to increase his own faith in God's protection. But even though his faith was strong, his spirit was heavy. Rudi was tired—tired of running, tired of the cold, tired of bleak winter forests.

CHAPTER TWENTY-TWO
A REFUGE
MAY 1943

Ye have heard that it hath been said, Thou shalt love thy neighbor, and hate thine enemy. But I say unto you, Love your enemies, bless them that curse you, do good to them that hate you, and pray for them which despitefully use you, and persecute you; That ye may be the children of your Father which is in heaven: for he maketh his sun to rise on the evil and on the good, and sendeth rain on the just and on the unjust.
—Matthew 5:43-45

It was spring. The forest was alive with green trees and brightly colored wildflowers. Four winters had passed since Rudi had found Ingrid. During that time, Rudi had been growing at an incredible rate. So fast, in fact, that sometimes he felt as if his large hands and feet belonged to someone else.

Ingrid had not been so fortunate. Although Rudi had done his best to see that she was well fed, it seemed that no amount of care could put much weight on her tiny frame. Nor had she grown much taller. Despite her slow growth, however, she had always seemed active and healthy until the last week or so when she developed a strange rash on her hands and feet. At first the rash seemed only to annoy her by causing a constant itching. Then she lost her appetite and grew restless at night. Rudi began to worry.

"Come on, Ingrid," he pleaded, as he placed some berries he had picked into her hand. "You really have to eat."

She took them listlessly but made no attempt to eat them.

"If you eat, I'll get you more drawing stones and make you some more pencils," he said, trying to tempt her.

Rudi had discovered Ingrid's passion for making pictures early in their time together, and he had tried to keep her supplied with smooth, light-colored stones and charred bark. The stones were a good substitute for paper, and the bark made excellent pencils. But now, even the promise of art supplies could not make her eat the few berries he had given to her.

She sat motionless, her toy rabbit draped carelessly across her knee. The plaything had taken quite a beating during their time together. It was so soiled and ragged that it could scarcely be identified as a rabbit any longer. Rudi had tried to take it from her once to wash it, but she protested so strongly that he finally gave up. It was their only real argument.

"I wish my father were here," he finally said, speaking more to himself than to Ingrid. "He'd be able to do something for you. Even Oscar would have been able to do more for you than I can now."

But the thought of Oscar brought another idea to mind. He remembered Anna. Maybe she could help. He had not been to see her since that night over three years ago when he and Oscar had parted. After the Germans had increased their threats, the villagers grew more fearful. Farmers began reporting their neighbors for housing or feeding Jews or resistance fighters. Rudi had heard of several villagers who had been shot because of such accusations. Although Anna's farm was more secluded than most, Rudi still hesitated to visit, mostly because of Josef. That boy could not be trusted.

But now as he looked at Ingrid, he began to reconsider. Maybe there was some way to go to Anna's without putting her in any danger. If Josef kept quiet, Rudi could pass off as Anna's hired help, for even if some of the other villagers did see him, he knew that they would not suspect that he was Jewish. And it was common for young Polish boys who had lost their families to drift from farm to farm, working for food and shelter. Maybe, just maybe, he could stay with her until Ingrid was well again. He could at least visit Anna and see what she thought of the idea. He was confident that she would be honest with him.

Even if she does advise us to return to the forest, he thought, *a visit will help. I can at least get some advice, and possibly some medicine, for Ingrid.*

When Anna opened the door, Rudi was somewhat startled. He had remembered her being much taller and more friendly. She did not seem particularly glad to see him.

"Hello, Anna," he said, then hesitated. "You said if I ever needed anything to—"

"Rudi!" she gasped, cutting him off. "Come in, come in," she urged, looking more and more as he remembered her. She motioned for them to come and sit down.

"You've certainly changed," she said and rushed about the kitchen, getting plates and food out of the cupboards.

"I guess I have," Rudi admitted as he sat down and lifted Ingrid up on his knee.

"And who's this?" Anna asked, as she set some bread before them.

"This is Ingrid," Rudi answered as he began to eat.

Anna smiled and bent forward to greet the little girl. "How do you do, Ingrid?"

"She doesn't talk," Rudi said between mouthfuls. "But believe me," he added with a smile, "she can let you know what she wants."

Rudi tried, without success, to get Ingrid to eat a piece of bread.

"She doesn't seem to have much spunk tonight," Anna observed.

"No," said Rudi. "That's why I've come. She's sick, Anna, and I don't know what to do. See her skin? It's getting all blotchy, and she's lost her appetite too. Doesn't want to sleep either."

Anna reached out and took her. Ingrid made no objection.

"Well, the first thing she needs is a good hot bath," Anna said as she cradled Ingrid in her lap. She glanced at Rudi. "And I think you could use one as well."

"I think you're right," said Rudi, and he felt the color rising in his cheeks.

She then leaned back in her chair and gave him a more thorough appraisal. "You could use a haircut and some new clothes as well."

"You should have seen my hair before now. It got so bad that I had to take a chance at visiting a farmer and convincing him to let me use his shears. As it turned out, his wife gave Ingrid and me some clothes as well."

"I still can't believe how much you've grown!" She gave her head a shake. "You must be at least a foot taller. It's a good thing you grew up faster than you grew out. Otherwise, you would've ripped those trousers to shreds."

Rudi laughed. "Haven't had a chance to look at myself much since I saw you last."

"Then it's time you did," said Anna. "I think you may be surprised. Go. There's a small mirror on the bureau over there."

Rudi went over to the bureau and picked up the mirror. He stood a moment, looking at the intricately carved handle, as if stalling for time. For some reason he was hesitant to bring the mirror up to his face. From Anna's reaction he was not so sure he wanted to see how he had changed.

What he did see completely astonished him. Aside from the fact that his hair was an absolutely matted mess, he could barely recognize his face. He was no longer a round-faced boy. His face was much thinner and more angular. His features were larger and his jaw strong. As he stood staring at himself, he realized that though he was fair like his mother, he looked more like his father than he had ever imagined possible.

"You've turned out to be quite a handsome young man," Anna said, "though you'll not be able to see that until you get cleaned up."

Rudi was still too dazed to comment.

She tried, unsuccessfully, to hide a smile. "If you can pull yourself away from that mirror, you might help me get your bath ready."

"Oh, sure. Sorry," Rudi said. He turned away from the mirror.

"Go into the next room there, and bring that large metal tub out here," Anna instructed him. "You'll find it behind the curtain."

Rudi obeyed.

"You're both going to need some new clothes," Anna was saying as Rudi reentered with the tub. "Those that you have on now will have to be burned."

"But this is all I have," he said. "And Ingrid doesn't have any other clothes either. I found her in a hayloft."

Anna looked indignant. "It's disgraceful the things helpless children are driven to these days," she said.

She stood several moments thinking, her hands resting firmly on her hips.

"I think I can find some for *you,*" she said. "I still have most of my husband's things, and you've grown enough to where they will fit you nicely, I think."

"Thank you," he said.

Anna walked over and collected the coat and scarf Rudi had removed as soon as he had entered the cottage. She gathered up Ingrid's coat as well.

"You can have my coat," he told her, "but you'd better leave the scarf."

Anna was firm. "It all goes."

"But it's not mine, Anna, it's Oscar's," he explained. "I don't mind you burning my clothes, but I'm not so sure about letting you burn his."

"Oscar's, is it?" Anna crossed the room and dropped the clothes just outside the door. "Well, when he returns and asks you for it, you just send him to me. I'll take care of him."

"I bet you will," said Rudi with a smile.

"It'll take me a bit more time to come up with something for Ingrid," she said. "I'll have to make her some. But until I can get to that I can certainly find something to at least wrap her up in."

"Well," said Rudi, "you've solved all the problems before I've even thought of them."

"Not all of them," said Anna, watching Ingrid carefully.

She motioned for Rudi to come close to her.

"That rabbit," she said, pointing at Ingrid's once-stuffed toy. "It will have to be burned with the clothes."

Rudi shook his head. "I think she'd rather let *me* go than that rabbit."

"I was afraid of that." Anna set a pot of water on the stove to heat. "Still, I'm afraid that rash of hers is infectious. That toy is too filthy to keep. For her own good, it has to go."

"Can't we wash it or something?" pleaded Rudi.

"I've thought of that," said Anna, "but it's so ragged now that it would never hold up under a decent scrubbing."

"I don't know, Anna. In all the time I've known her she hasn't let that thing out of her sight."

But Anna was firm on the point. "Do you want to speak to her or shall I?" she asked.

Ingrid sat looking at them both from across the room. Rudi could tell that she sensed something was wrong. He had found long ago that there was no hiding things from her.

"Listen, Ingrid," he began as he walked over to the table and pulled a chair close to hers. "Your rabbit—it's, well, it's awfully dirty."

She looked at him suspiciously, then drew the ragged toy closer to her.

Rudi took a deep breath and then continued. "We think it may be what's making you sick. We're going to have to—well, put it away."

Her lower lip began to tremble, and she turned her face from him.

"Look, Ingrid," he said, "you know I'd never take it from you if I didn't have to. It's just that I love you. I don't want you to be sick. You understand that, don't you?"

He reached out and gently took the rabbit from her. She did not fight him—which in some ways only made it worse for him. Instead of fighting, she simply gave up. Then, sliding down from her chair, she went over to the corner of the room.

Rudi handed the toy to Anna and followed Ingrid. She stood facing the wall so that Rudi could not see her face. Still, he could tell by her very posture that she felt betrayed. He reached out to her and took her hand, but she drew back from him.

He looked to Anna, who stood holding the toy.

"I'll be right back," she said and left without further explanation.

Rudi continued kneeling beside Ingrid, feeling absolutely wretched until Anna returned.

When she entered, she no longer held the rabbit, but in its place she had a puppy. It was the prettiest dog he had ever seen. She brought the dog to Rudi and handed it to him. It was small enough to lie comfortably along his forearm and hand, its front legs dangling down on either side. It was as white as snow and had bright blue eyes. As he took it, it gave him a friendly swipe on the face with its lolling tongue.

"What kind is it?" he whispered.

"A sledge dog—a malemute," Anna said, no longer talking softly. "I got rid of all the pups but this one; I couldn't part with it. At least, not until I found someone who'd love it and take care of it."

Rudi turned again to Ingrid. "Ingrid, here's something for you. It's not a rabbit, but it needs someone to care for it."

She turned only slightly, but enough to catch a glimpse of the dog.

"Does it have a name?" Rudi asked.

"I call her Sasha," Anna replied.

Rudi put Sasha down beside Ingrid. The pup moved over and licked Ingrid's boots. After this initial "inspection," Sasha decided it was safe to sit on Ingrid's feet. Once comfortably settled, she began to rub her nose against the little girl's legs.

"See, she doesn't want me to take care of her. She wants you to," Rudi told Ingrid.

Ingrid looked down at the soft white ball of fur. After a moment's hesitation, she leaned over and tried to hold the puppy in her hands.

Rudi breathed a sigh of relief. The crisis was over.

"It feels great to be clean!" said Rudi as he set some plates on the table for dinner. "Thanks for the haircut, too," he added, returning for more dishes.

"You needn't thank me," Anna laughed. "I only helped you clean up out of self-defense."

Rudi took the bantering good-naturedly. "In any case, it has helped. Even Ingrid's perked up a bit now that she's had a bath and all. Look, she's even hungry—she's got her fingers in the cheese," he said, taking the cups Anna had given him.

"Yes, she does," said Anna. "But you notice she's not the one eating it."

Rudi turned. Sure enough, Ingrid was taking hunks of cheese from the plate and feeding them to Sasha.

"Well," he said, "at least the dog's got a good appetite. I still think Ingrid's feeling better though, don't you? Maybe a good bath was all that she needed."

"I think the bath helped," said Anna. "I also put some ointment on her. But it'll be a few days before we know for sure if she needs something more." Seeing Rudi's concern, she added, "I'm sure she'll be fine in a week or two, though."

"By the way," Rudi asked as they sat down to dinner, "where's Josef?"

"Haven't seen him in several months," Anna said.

"What happened? Did you two have an argument or something?"

Anna laughed. "Rudi, you should remember enough about Josef to know that everyone argued with him. I don't think he'd pick a fight with you now, though. You're probably a good head taller that he is, and I assure you, he is not a brave boy. As to why he left, to be honest, I don't know for sure, though I have my suspicions. I know only that he's gone to Warsaw."

"Why in the world would he want to go into the city?" Rudi asked. "He was much better off here—plenty to eat and a warm place to sleep. Anna, Warsaw was awful when I left it four years ago. People were starving to death then. I'm sure it hasn't gotten any better."

She looked at him with a curious expression. "Most of the people were starving, Rudi. But I'll wager that there were others who knew how to fill their bellies and make a profit besides."

"The only people I saw with 'full bellies' were the Germans," Rudi answered.

"And the Poles who'd work for them," Anna added.

"I didn't know anybody like that," Rudi said.

"Of course you didn't," Anna said. "First of all, I doubt your father was the kind of man to know such people, and if he did, I doubt he would have let you associate with them. Besides, you must remember that you left Warsaw only months after the takeover. The Gestapo hadn't had time to stir up enough ruckus to make the rats come running out of their holes."

Rudi frowned. "No Pole would help a Nazi."

"You forget Josef."

"Josef's just stupid. He talks like he would, but if he'd been in the city and seen what they were like, he would change his mind all right."

"Then why does he stay in the city?" asked Anna.

Rudi hesitated. "I can't answer that," he finally said.

"I believe I can," Anna told him. "I think he's doing some spying for the Nazis and getting a good price for it."

"What kind of spying?" asked Rudi.

"Oh, like finding Jews who have gone into hiding to escape deportation. The Germans pay well for such information."

"I'm telling you, Anna, not even Josef could do such a thing—not once he'd seen the Nazis in action," said Rudi.

Anna's voice was almost sharp. "Do you think that the Nazis are the only men who are cruel?"

Her look and her voice made him feel a little foolish. "Of course not! But they are the worst."

"I see," said Anna. "The Poles, the French, the English, the Americans—they could not be so bad?"

"No," said Rudi.

"You're wrong, Rudi," she said. "You know I have not always been a farm girl. I grew up in the city. My father's business often took him to other parts of Europe, and a few times the family went along with him. We went to France twice and England once. Do you know what I found, Rudi? I found that there are good—and bad—men everywhere."

Rudi sat staring down at his plate.

"You don't believe me," she said.

"I believe you, Anna," Rudi finally admitted. "As a matter of fact, I was just thinking how much like my father you sounded."

"Ah, yes, your father," Anna said. "Oscar told me of him, a good man. And always right too," she added, smiling.

"Most always," Rudi said.

"Tell me," said Anna, "what would your father say?"

Rudi smiled. "He would say: 'Rudi, men are not evil because they follow Hitler. They follow Hitler because they are evil, because they refuse the grace of God.' And he would remind me that apart from God's grace, I could be just as they are."

"Do you believe that?" Anna asked.

Rudi hesitated a moment. "Yes," he finally said. "The things that I have seen during this war have made me very angry, Anna. So angry that I have at times been filled with hate."

"You have a right to be angry, and even to hate at times," she said. "I am certain even a man like your father would agree."

"Yes," said Rudi, "he'd agree that I should hate the evil and even that I should do all in my power to fight it. But he'd also tell me that I must fight because I love the good, not because I hate men."

"It's hard to separate the men from the evil they do. Are you able to do that?" asked Anna.

He had to hesitate on that. "I know that I love the good," he faltered.

"Then you are farther than most men," said Anna.

Although Anna was satisfied with his growth, Rudi knew that neither his earthly father nor his heavenly Father would be. They would not be satisfied until his heart was pure enough to hate evil without hating evil men. And he had an uneasy feeling that there would soon come a time when God would try him to see indeed what kind of heart he had.

CHAPTER TWENTY-THREE
JOSEF'S RETURN
MAY 1944

The discretion of a man deferreth his anger; and it is his glory to pass over a transgression.

—Proverbs 19:11

The months they had spent at Anna's had been so peaceful that it almost seemed as if the war had ceased. Rudi loved his work on the farm, and he felt sure that, with his Swedish looks, he did not arouse the suspicions of those few people who passed by now and then. Also, Ingrid was doing much better. Under Anna's care she not only grew healthier but also learned to read and write. Her drawing improved too. But despite Anna's and Rudi's urgings, Ingrid would use nothing but bark pencils and smooth stones for her art. So Rudi continued collecting them for her each morning.

Sasha, Ingrid's constant companion, had also grown. She was no longer a pudgy ball of fur but rather a strong, muscular dog. Although she was fierce enough to terrify any passing stranger, she permitted Ingrid to subject her to all kinds of playful indignities without the slightest objection. She was completely submissive to Ingrid. One incident, however, showed Rudi that Sasha's submissiveness did not extend to the other members of the household.

As usual Rudi had gotten up at dawn, milked the cows, then taken them out into the fields to graze. About mid-morning, Ingrid and Sasha joined him. Since the cows needed to graze at least two more hours, Rudi decided that he would teach Sasha some tricks while they waited.

Teaching her to sit seemed to be a good place to start. He had a rope with him that he used as a kind of leash whenever he needed to coax a stubborn cow into moving. Taking this rope, he tied it loosely around Sasha's neck. He then gave the leash a slight upward tug, and at the same time he gently pushed down on her hind quarters. "Sit," he said. She looked up at him dumbly. He decided to try another tack.

"Sit," he repeated. And this time as he spoke, he not only gave the leash an upward tug but also tried to gently but firmly buckle Sasha's hind legs under her. Still, she stood firm, and her innocent appearance looked less convincing.

"Come on, Sasha," Rudi urged. "You're supposed to be a smart dog."

For the next hour or two he tried patiently to get her to master the simple task. At last he left off pleading and resorted to yelling. He even tried bribing her with some of the cheese Anna had given him for a snack. But nothing seemed to work. Ingrid had been carefully watching the whole charade.

"Sorry, Ingrid," Rudi finally said, slipping the rope off Sasha's neck. "Your dog may be pretty, but she's just too dumb to train. Come on, let's get these cows rounded up and head back to the cottage for lunch."

After several steps, however, he realized that Ingrid was not following him. He turned to see her standing over Sasha. Her look was stern. So stern, in fact, that Sasha laid down flat on the ground, her head on her forepaws. Rudi almost burst out laughing as he saw Sasha stare mournfully up at Ingrid.

Ingrid stood several moments, hands on hips, glaring down at the dog. During this reprimand, the only movement poor Sasha made was to let one ear point upward. But as soon as Ingrid shook her finger, the ear immediately resumed its former position—flat against the husky's head.

Rudi was just about to herd the cows toward the cottage again when Ingrid changed her tactic. She ceased her reprimand and smiled down at Sasha. Such approval put Sasha on her feet in a moment. Then Ingrid patted Sasha's hind quarters. To Rudi's astonishment, the silly dog not only sat down but also remained as still as a statue until Ingrid motioned for her to follow. From that time on Rudi knew that he had no choice but to leave Sasha's training to Ingrid.

Rudi had just finished getting the cows back to the barn when he saw a stranger approaching. Sasha left Ingrid's side to rush to the edge of the road. Taking a threatening stance, she bared her teeth and dared the stranger to enter without welcome.

Rudi ran to the dog and took her by the scruff of the neck. Anna had come out to see what was causing the commotion, and she and Ingrid now stood waiting in the doorway. Holding the dog tightly, Rudi strained to see the stranger in the distance. Whoever it was seemed to ignore Sasha's warning and continued on at a steady pace. As the man drew near, Rudi began to sense that there was something familiar in the stranger's gait, but he walked with his head down, and Rudi could not see his face. Finally he looked up. It was Josef.

He passed Rudi without speaking. Walking straight up to Anna he said, "I'm hungry. Fix me something to eat."

"You will eat with the rest of us," she said, "and that will not be until the chores are finished."

He glared but did not contradict her. They both disappeared into the cottage.

Rudi had not liked the tone of his voice. Neither had Sasha. And it now took all of his strength to hold her back.

"It's all right, Sasha," he said, comforting her, though he did not speak with much assurance.

Josef's return completely altered the atmosphere of the house. Over the next few days, Anna became solemn. Ingrid was inattentive at her lessons, and Sasha became more like a caged wolf than a pet. She would not even play with Ingrid. All her attention was given to watching Josef. When he was in the house, she prowled about, watching his every move. When he went outside, she followed. And even when he lay down to sleep, she lay down a few feet from him, barely allowing her head to drop down and rest on her forepaws.

Rudi had determined to keep his distance. He had no desire to fight. Although after seeing Josef, Rudi agreed with Anna: in a fight Rudi would definitely have the upper hand. It was a comforting thought. Rudi's present concern was that such odds would not be enough to confine Josef's hatred indefinitely. He was right.

"Well," said Josef one evening as they all sat down to dinner, "I think I'll be heading back to Warsaw in the morning. I'm sure you're all grieved to hear that."

"We'd be glad to have your company, Josef, if you worked a little more at being pleasant," said Anna. "As

I've told you before, it's not you I object to—it's your sour disposition."

"I would think you'd be better off here anyway," said Rudi, trying to be pleasant. "I have heard that there is a great deal of unrest in the city."

"Not any longer," said Josef. "Besides," he continued, casting a glance at Ingrid and Rudi, "I think I may have some information to give the authorities there."

Rudi's anger flared, but he tried to give no visible indication of it.

"I hope," said Anna firmly, "you are not thinking of trying to stir up trouble here."

"Here, Aunt Anna?" Josef said. "Why should there be trouble here? It's not unusual for farmers to allow little orphaned Polish boys to help them with the chores. And some would think you very noble to take on an orphan girl who could be of absolutely no use at all."

"No," said Rudi, "it's not any more unusual to hire 'little Polish boys' on the farm than it is to allow little Polish farm boys to go into the city and play spy."

Anna put down her fork. "There will be no arguing at my table," she said.

"I'm sorry," said Rudi.

Anna waited for Josef's apology. It did not come. Rudi was tempted to pick him up by the scruff of the neck and shake it out of him, but out of deference to Anna he went on with his meal.

Josef continued the conversation as if there had been no disagreement. "Tell me, Rudi," he said, "how did you, being way out here, hear that there was unrest in Warsaw?"

"We do some trading with the other farms," said Rudi sullenly. "The farmers speak of it." He changed his strategy. "They also say that the Germans are no longer winning the war. Not only do they face unrest here in Warsaw, but they are also losing ground abroad. Now that the

Americans have joined the Allies, the Allies are regaining strength. The Germans, on the other hand, are said to be losing on nearly every field—especially in Russia."

"Don't believe everything you hear," Josef snarled. "Don't the Germans still have control of Denmark, Norway, and all of the Low Countries—not to mention France? Those facts hardly indicate their weakness. And as for this unrest in Warsaw, I can guarantee that an uprising would be no more successful than the one staged last year."

"There was one last year?" asked Rudi, unable to conceal his interest.

"Oh, yes," said Josef. "I'm surprised you did not hear of that one. It was started by the Jews."

Josef watched Rudi's reaction to his comments carefully, and he was glad to see that the news obviously troubled him.

"A Jewish uprising," Rudi repeated, his thoughts going immediately to Salek and his parents.

"Yes, that's what I said," Josef said acidly. "Unfortunately, several German soldiers were killed."

"How many Jews?" demanded Rudi.

"Jews?" said Josef. "Oh, I imagine there were hundreds; those who were not killed were sent off to camps. But what should that matter?" he asked, smiling.

"I would say a great deal," said Rudi, "for Scripture says that those who touch the Jews touch the apple of God's eye."

"Rather a rotten apple, I should say," said Josef. "A few Jews more or less don't matter."

Anna started to light into Josef, but Rudi beat her to it. "To someone with as little sense as you have, I don't imagine that the number of Jews killed would be of any interest," said Rudi. He then tried to regain his composure, for he wanted more information. "But since the Germans in your opinion are, shall we say, 'worth' more, perhaps you could recall the names of some of the soldiers killed."

"Yes, yes I can," said Josef. "There was a man named Schmidt, another named Heinrich, and—yes, a rather important officer named Mende."

Josef noted Rudi's reaction at the mention of Mende.

"You knew one of them?"

"I have heard of Mende," Rudi said.

"A great man," said Josef, trying once again to goad Rudi into fighting.

Rudi made no reply to Josef's comment.

"That's enough, Josef," said Anna.

"Why are you so upset, Aunt Anna? Rudi wants information, and I'm giving it to him," he said. Then turning back to Rudi he added, "I've heard of the things Mende did to Jews," said Josef. "He was quite creative. Would you like to hear some of his techniques of interrogation?"

"No," said Rudi before Anna could say more. "To be quite frank, Josef, your conversation bores me. You don't have any opinions of your own. As a matter of fact, I've never heard you make one original comment. You only repeat what you have read on propaganda posters."

Now Josef grew angry. "What are you insinuating?"

"I'm not insinuating anything," said Rudi. "I'm simply telling you that I enjoy talking to people, not to parrots. So if you don't mind, why don't you let Anna talk awhile."

The insult went home, and Josef—in frustration—could think of nothing to say.

Seeing that Rudi had the best end of the argument, Anna seemed content. Rudi pretended not to see either Josef's anger or Anna's approval. He simply waited for Josef to make his usual raging exit and leave them in peace for the night.

Instead of storming out, Josef jumped up from his seat and reached for Rudi. In doing so, he made a serious mistake, for he had to lean over Ingrid to get at Rudi.

Without warning Sasha leaped from her resting place. The force of her body knocked Josef from his feet, and in a moment Sasha was on him. Rudi, fearing that Sasha would kill Josef, nearly jumped over the table to take Sasha by the neck. It took all of his strength to hold her.

"Get her off me!" Josef cried. "Get her off!"

Rudi had never seen such fear, and as he looked down at his enemy, he lost all desire for vengeance. Still, he did not think it wise to let Josef know his feeling. It was a good chance to teach him a lesson. Thus, Rudi stood a moment more, letting Josef feel the dog's breath against his cheek and see her bared teeth at close range. "It is a frightening thing to have a dog attack you, isn't it? I hear that Mende liked to set dogs on to Jews—one of his techniques you were talking about. It is fortunate for you that I am not the kind of person he was."

Having made his point, Rudi pulled Sasha back.

Josef got up trembling and turned to his aunt. "I'll be leaving in the morning, so have a good breakfast for me." Then turning to Rudi he added, "I'll sleep in the barn tonight. Make sure you keep that dog away from me!" And he stomped out and slammed the door.

"I like his sense of gratitude," said Rudi to Anna, trying to lighten things up a bit.

"Thank you, Rudi," she said quietly. "You're a good boy—a good boy."

CHAPTER TWENTY-FOUR
A HARD DECISION
MAY 1944

Hear my prayer, O God; give ear to the words of my mouth. For strangers are risen up against me, and oppressors seek after my soul: they have not set God before them. Behold, God is mine helper: the Lord is with them that uphold my soul.

—Psalm 54:2-4

Rudi lay in bed enjoying the night, unwilling to let it pass. He knew what he must do. He knew, too, that he had put it off too long and that he could not afford to wait. Reluctantly he got up and went quietly into the room where Ingrid and Anna slept.

"Anna," he whispered.

She stirred but did not awaken.

Fearing that he would disturb Ingrid as well, he went to Anna's side of the bed and leaned over to touch her arm. She opened her eyes.

"Anna, we have to talk," he said.

"What time is it?" she asked him.

"Late," he said.

"Can't it wait until morning?" she asked. But she sat up.

"No," he replied. "I don't think so."

"All right," she said. "Go out and put the kettle on the stove for some tea. I'll be along as soon as I can get the sleep out of my eyes."

Rudi had just finished straining the tea and pouring it into the pitcher when Anna appeared in the kitchen.

"Got it all ready for you," he said as he placed two cups on the table and then returned to get the pitcher.

"Whatever's on your mind must be important for you to get me out of bed for tea at this hour," she said.

He sat down across from her. "It is."

"It's got something to do with Josef, doesn't it?"

"Yes," said Rudi. "I don't want another incident like the one we had earlier this evening."

"There shouldn't be. He's leaving tomorrow," Anna said.

"He may be leaving," said Rudi, "but if I stay here, I assure you he'll be back to stir up trouble."

"What kind of trouble?"

Rudi hesitated. "I think he is considering telling the Germans that you are giving refuge to a Jew."

"No, Rudi," Anna argued, "he's just talking. He has no idea you're Jewish! He wasn't around when Oscar told me."

"I think he does," Rudi said. "I think he's known ever since that first night I came here with Oscar. He almost got a rise out of me even then, remember?"

"Well even if that's true, what makes you think that your leaving will help matters any? The Nazis wouldn't care if you were still here. If they thought I'd given you refuge, they would take me away all the same."

"I don't think Josef'll tell them if I leave," said Rudi. "He may be rude to you—he's rude to everybody—but he bears you no real grudge. He hates me, however. If I leave here, I take away the motive for his betrayal."

"Maybe we can think of something else," said Anna hopefully.

"I'm afraid not, Anna," Rudi said. "Believe me, I have been trying all day and most of the night to come up with something. This is it."

They both sat in silence for a while, slowly drinking their tea.

"You know, Anna," Rudi said after several minutes, "I've never quite been able to figure out why Josef hates me so much. I know it's not just the fact that I'm a Jew, because he hated me from the moment he first laid eyes on me. I remember the look he gave me the very first time you introduced us."

"I think he hates you, Rudi, because you are what he is not," Anna said.

"What do you mean?" asked Rudi.

She looked thoughtful. "Well, I guess I mean that you are easy to like."

"Well, Josef could be if he'd change," Rudi said.

She shook her head. "He doesn't believe that. He believes that the problem is not with him but with those around him. Take the soldiers, for example. They seemed to take you in and approve of you immediately, but they never paid any attention to Josef," she said.

"Well, what did he expect," asked Rudi, "when he made all those pro-German speeches?"

"He didn't talk like that from the beginning. In fact, he never talked that way until after the resistance group had met here for several months, and I think that it began simply because he wanted some attention. He couldn't get it from the men in an acceptable manner, so he began to goad them and fight with them. It worked."

"I should say."

"Then you show up," she continued. "They let you eat with them and listen to their talk as if you were a part of them. He felt cheated. He had to fight for attention; you just came in and sat down."

"You know that was only because of Oscar," Rudi said.

"Sure, I know that, but he didn't."

"Why didn't you say something to the men?" asked Rudi.

"Well, I didn't really figure it out until sometime later. By then it was too late. Josef had already convinced himself that to fight for Germany was the answer. What he really wanted was approval, and I bet the Germans in Warsaw gave him that." She looked troubled.

"They're only using him," said Rudi.

"You and I know that, but—" she threw her arms up in a helpless gesture and then growing angry said, "he is just being stupid."

Rudi nodded. "Stupidity seems to be running rampant these days. You know, Anna, it is hard to understand how people can blindly follow wicked men. Hitler has convinced thousands that the Jews are thieves and murderers, and he is using fools to carry out his own hatred."

"And it is seldom easy to convince a person that he is playing the fool," said Anna.

"But for people to believe that it is right to hate an entire race of people. Take my best friend, Salek—he is a Jew. My father and his were best friends too. All of the Serduseks are good people. They—" he hesitated. "I will never find another friend like Salek, Anna, never." He could say no more.

Anna placed her hand upon his arm. "Maybe you won't have to find another friend. Don't lose hope, Rudi."

"I only wish I knew if they were among those killed in the Jewish uprising."

"Would it really help to know right now?" she asked.

"I don't know."

"Even Josef admitted that many of the Jews were not killed but sent to camps," she said, trying to encourage him. "Maybe the Serduseks are at the camps. Maybe they were even sent to the same one your father was sent to."

"Maybe," Rudi said, but there was little conviction in his voice.

"Besides, if Salek is like you, he will survive," she said.

"I pray that that is so, Anna," Rudi said. "Every day I pray that it is so."

"Then to lose hope would mean to lose faith, wouldn't it?" she asked him.

Rudi smiled. "Yes, I suppose it would, and I of all people should know better. God has been so faithful to me, Anna."

"And He will continue to be," she said. "Now, you tell me you must go," she continued. "When do you plan to leave?"

"I should leave just after dawn," Rudi replied.

"What about Ingrid? Is she to go with you?"

"What do you think?"

"You have taken good care of her, Rudi," Anna said, "and I know that you two could not love each other more if you were family. Therefore, it must be your decision."

Rudi wanted more than anything to take Ingrid with him, but he needed some assurance that it was best for her. He needed Anna's sanction.

"Just tell me honestly, Anna, what would you do if you were me?" he asked her.

"If I were you, Rudi, I would have grown weary of saying good-bye to those I love, and I would avoid having to say another. I am afraid I would take her with me."

"Afraid? Why afraid?" asked Rudi.

"Because that would be a decision of the heart and not the head."

"You do not think that it is best for her then," said Rudi, disappointed.

"The forest is not the place for a little girl. She is not strong like you, Rudi," said Anna. "Though I believe with all my heart that, if you take her, you will give all the protection you can."

Rudi suddenly felt very tired. "She will stay with you," he said.

"Do you want to say good-bye to her?" asked Anna.

"No," said Rudi quickly. Then he added, "I will let you tell her that I've gone away. Make sure that she knows that it is just for a while. Make sure she knows that I will be back for her."

"Are you certain you must go?"

"Yes," he said. "I will leave in a couple of hours."

"Then I must get busy. There is much to do and little time."

"You need not do anything, Anna. I travel light, and I'll have no trouble finding something to eat by lunchtime," Rudi assured her.

"Well, I will at least pack you an extra set of clothes. That way you will always be able to have clean things to wear. This time when you return I want to see you before I smell you."

Rudi laughed outright.

"Do I have to keep my hair cut as well?" he asked her.

"No," she said, smiling. "You see I have a feeling that you will be able to return before you need another haircut."

"I hope you're right," said Rudi.

"Why don't you get an hour or so more sleep? There is time," Anna urged.

"No," said Rudi. "I have a couple of things I need to do."

"At this hour?" asked Anna. "What do you need to be doing at this hour?"

"Well, I thought I'd make a few more bark pencils for Ingrid. I'll go out and collect as many smooth stones as I can too. You know Ingrid, she's a finicky artist."

"I've never seen such a child," said Anna. "Think what she could do if she were willing to use pencil and paper instead of stones and bark."

"I'm confident that I'll be able to convince her of it someday," said Rudi.

"Is that all you have to do before going?" asked Anna.

"No, there's one more thing," he said.

"Is it something I can help you with?" she asked.

"No, not this time," he said. "I'm just planning to have a little chat with Josef on my way out."

"What do you plan to tell him?"

"Oh," said Rudi, "let's just say that I intend to put a bit of fear into his heart. Just enough to make him think twice before he comes around again. Or before he sends anyone else to visit you."

"That will have to be some speech," said Anna.

"It will be," Rudi said.

Having given Anna Ingrid's "art supplies" and said his farewell, he headed for the barn. Although he felt more melancholy than argumentative, he knew that in all likelihood he would have to steel himself for a fight. Josef would probably still be sleeping, and Rudi doubted that he would enjoy being awakened. He was ill-tempered enough in midday. Rudi could hardly wait to see how he would be when first awakened in the morning.

Rudi entered the barn and called out to him. There was no answer for some time. Eventually, however, he heard someone moving in the loft.

"What do you want," said Josef.

Rudi looked up.

"Come down here and I'll tell you," Rudi said.

"Why should I bother?" asked Josef.

"Because I'm sure you don't want me to have to come up there and get you," answered Rudi, growing more irritated by the moment.

Although he had saved Josef from Sasha, he still could not like the boy, for Rudi had never met anyone who could irritate him faster or keep him worked up longer.

Josef stood at the edge of the loft, glaring down at Rudi. Rudi waited quietly. His patience soon paid off. Josef descended the ladder.

"I'm here now. What is it you want?"

"I just wanted to tell you I'm leaving—"

"How sad," Josef interrupted.

Rudi ignored the comment. "But I assure you, I will be close by."

"That's convenient," said Josef.

"That is precisely my point," said Rudi. "I will be close enough to make certain that you do not disturb Anna or Ingrid."

"You can do nothing to stop me, Jew boy," said Josef.

"I would not test that theory if I were you," said Rudi. "I may have saved your life once, but I assure you that does not mean that I would not break your neck in a moment if you try to harm those I love."

"You may not be alive to do anything about it," Josef threatened.

Rudi laughed scornfully. "No German could find me once I get into the forest. I have grown far too cunning for them. So don't bother sending them after me."

As soon as Rudi's back was turned, however, he heard Josef moving. Instinctively Rudi turned again to face him, just in time to dodge the flying pitchfork Josef had heaved at him.

Enraged, Rudi charged Josef and pinned him to the wall.

"You are the biggest fool I have ever met!" he shouted angrily.

"You're choking me," gasped Josef.

"At this moment, I don't really care," said Rudi. And he kept his arm firmly placed across Josef's throat as he continued.

"Now you listen to me, and you listen carefully. I am confident that I shall live to see the end of this war. Do you know why, Josef? Because God has promised this Jew that He will keep him. You don't have any such promises, do you?"

"Stop choking me," pleaded Josef, genuine fear coming into his eyes.

Rudi loosened his grip only slightly.

"I saved your life once, but that does not mean I will let you get away with hurting those I love. I *will* do what I must to protect them. I'm leaving, but I'm not going far. And I warn you, Josef, if anything happens to Ingrid or Anna, or if so much as one blade of grass is damaged on this farm, I will be back for you. And I assure you, there are not enough Nazis in all of Europe to hide you from me. God will see to it. Do you understand?"

Josef nodded.

"Good," he said as he released his hold.

Josef slid down the wall, holding his throat and coughing. Rudi picked up his gear and left him, certain that he had put enough fear in Josef's heart to keep Ingrid and Anna safe.

CHAPTER TWENTY-FIVE
THE PASSING OF NIGHT
MAR. 1945

He shall deliver thee in six troubles: yea, in seven there shall no evil touch thee. In famine he shall redeem thee from death: and in war from the power of the sword.
—Job 5:19, 20

Rudi awakened to the rumbling sounds of heavy vehicles in the distance. Such sounds should not have seemed unusual, but the woods had been strangely quiet for the last several weeks. He decided to go see if he could discern how close the trouble really was.

Cautiously he ventured out into the field. As he did, he saw a farmer running, though he could see nothing behind the man that would make him flee.

As the man came closer, Rudi heard him shouting.

"The Huns are on the run! They're on the run!" he yelled to no one in particular, for no one but Rudi was about, and Rudi knew that the farmer had not caught sight of him yet. Abandoning all caution, Rudi rushed out to meet the man.

"Hey," he called to him, "hey, what was that you said?"

The man stopped and shouted once again.

"They're on the run, I tell you," he laughed. "The Germans are getting licked everywhere."

"How do you know that?" said Rudi, growing skeptical.

"Listen!" he shouted. "Can't you hear it?"

"I've heard those sounds plenty of times," said Rudi, "and it never meant that the Germans were losing before."

"Well, if you don't believe what you hear," the farmer said, "maybe you'll believe what you read."

Reaching into his back pocket, he pulled out a crumbled newspaper.

"Look at this," he said, waving the paper in Rudi's face.

Rudi grabbed it from him, for it was impossible to read with the man flapping it in front of him.

"RED ARMY ADVANCES INTO POLAND," the headlines read.

"Then the Russians are really coming to liberate Poland?" asked Rudi.

"Not coming," said the man. "They're here! That paper there is weeks old!"

The old man was nearly dancing a jig, while Rudi stood as if he were frozen to the ground. He was afraid to move, afraid that if he did, he would awaken and find that he was dreaming.

"I tell you, Warsaw has been liberated! All of Poland is free!" the old man said.

Rudi still said nothing.

"What's wrong with you, boy? Can't you hear what I'm saying?"

"I hear you, I hear you," Rudi assured him. "It's just— well, it's almost too good to be true."

"It's true all right," the man said, slapping Rudi on the back. "Those Germans are fleeing for their lives, and I'm going to run all over this countryside shouting it until everybody knows!"

With these parting words, he was off again waving his newspaper in the air and yelling.

"It's over," Rudi said to himself. "I can't believe it, but it's really over."

The old man's voice had barely faded out of range when Rudi heard more voices. He looked up to see a small group of men approaching, and he could see that some of them wore uniforms.

"Soldiers," he said, his caution returning. "Well, they're not going to get me this close to the end." He was about to take to his heels when he saw that the soldiers had no guns. There were four men behind them, however, who did. These men were dressed in tattered clothes. Rudi realized that the Germans had been taken captive. He was uncertain, however, whether the captors were Polish or Russian.

"Keep them moving, boys," one of the men with a gun shouted.

Rudi was startled, for he thought he recognized the voice. He waited eagerly, hoping the man would speak again.

"We haven't far to go now," the man said.

As soon as Rudi heard the voice a second time, he took off running toward him.

"Oscar!" Rudi cried. "Oscar!"

Oscar turned quickly and aimed the gun at him.

Rudi stopped.

"Put that down," he called to him. "It's me, Rudi."

Oscar's stern face broke into a smile. He left his men with the prisoners and came running up to meet Rudi.

"I thought I taught you never to startle a man who's carrying a gun," Oscar scolded. "I can see you still have a lot to learn."

Rudi willingly took the rebuke. He understood that a reprimand was Oscar's idea of a friendly greeting.

Oscar then stood back to look Rudi over carefully. "I say, you certainly have grown! And where'd you get fitted out in such fancy clothes? Those aren't the ones you had on the last time I saw you."

"Anna gave them to me," said Rudi.

"By the way, where's my scarf?" Oscar asked cheerfully.

"Well," Rudi hesitated, "Anna burned it."

"Burned it!" Oscar, genuinely indignant, stepped back. "What in the world did you let her do that for?"

"Oscar, you know once Anna sets her mind to something, even *you* can't change it," Rudi told him. "How in the world did you expect me to stop her?"

Oscar had to agree. "But what in the world possessed her to do a thing like that anyway?" he asked.

"It *was* awfully dirty," Rudi said.

"Women!" Oscar said. Then he added rather pitifully, "She could have washed it instead of burning it."

Rudi could not help smiling. "No," he said, "I have to stick up for her there. It wouldn't have done any good to wash it. I'd been wearing it for over three years by the time she got to it. And who knows how long you had had it."

"Three years? You mean you didn't go back to see her for three whole years?"

"I was afraid to," said Rudi. He was rather relieved that Oscar had finally gotten off the subject of the scarf. "Things got really bad around here for a while," he explained. "The Germans were going about burning the villages of anyone who helped either a Jew or a Polish soldier. I didn't want to risk it, especially since Josef seemed so pro-German."

"What changed your mind?" asked Oscar.

"Well, it's a rather long story," said Rudi.

Oscar stood waiting, so Rudi continued.

"Right after I left you, I found a little girl in a hayloft. You know you used to tell me about children who slept in lofts and begged their food. Anyway, she was three, maybe four, when I found her. I took her with me and took care of her. We got along fine—"

"Thanks to all I'd taught you," interrupted Oscar.

"True," said Rudi. "At any rate, after about three years, she got sick—some kind of rash. I waited awhile, hoping it would just go away, but of course, it didn't. I had no idea what to do, so I took her to Anna."

"Anna fixed her up, I'm sure," said Oscar.

"Yes, she did," said Rudi. "I stayed on with her for a year, helping around the farm."

Oscar looked surprised. "Josef didn't object?"

"He wasn't around at first. He'd gone to Warsaw."

Oscar was immediately suspicious. "What for? The Poles were suffering terribly under the Germans there."

"Not if you played up to the Germans," Rudi said.

"That idiot!" shouted Oscar.

"Anyway," continued Rudi, "he came back to the farm after a few months."

"Why?" asked Oscar.

"Some kind of unrest in the city," said Rudi.

Oscar laughed a mirthless laugh. "I see. A coward as well as an idiot."

"He didn't stay long," said Rudi. "He headed back as soon as he'd heard things were under control again. I left the same time he did. I thought it would be safer for Anna."

"Do you think he informed the German authorities that you'd been there?" asked Oscar. "That wouldn't help Anna any, you know."

"Not a chance," said Rudi. "Like you said, he's a coward, and I threatened him within an inch of his life."

Oscar smiled.

"I've also been keeping an eye on the place from a distance," Rudi added. "Things are fine."

"Well, you don't have to worry anymore," said Oscar. "We've finally rousted the enemy—at least the German enemy. As for Josef, well, he'd better not show his face around there while I'm there."

"Is it true, then?" asked Rudi. "Are the Germans really done for?"

"They're done for all right," Oscar said. "They're fleeing toward Germany as fast as they can. But it won't do any good. We'll chase them right into their homeland!"

"Then it's safe to go back to Warsaw?" asked Rudi.

"I don't see why not," answered Oscar. "I'm sure there have been Russian troops on these roads for several days now. Surely, you've seen them."

"Now, how would I see them?" asked Rudi. "As I recall the man who taught me to survive in the forest told me repeatedly to stay deep in the woods during the daylight hours."

"That didn't seem to stop you today," said Oscar, feigning disapproval.

"You've got me there," admitted Rudi. "By the way, have the prisoners from the camps been released?"

Oscar's expression changed. "Many of them, yes," he said.

"You didn't happen to hear anything about my father did you?"

"No," said Oscar. "But—" he hesitated.

"But what?" asked Rudi.

"The camps, well—" he stopped again.

"Come on, Oscar, out with it," demanded Rudi.

"Don't get your hopes up, Rudi," he said.

"What do you mean?" asked Rudi.

"I mean that the German camps were not exactly work camps."

Rudi could feel his stomach knotting up.

"What were they, then?" he asked.

"They were more like death camps," said Oscar. "Many, many people died—especially Jews."

"But not all?"

"No, not all."

"Then I won't lose hope," said Rudi.

"I can't blame you for that," Oscar said.

"God kept me, Oscar," Rudi said. "He could've kept my father as well."

Oscar sighed. "Maybe." But his tone sounded skeptical. "Even if your father is alive, it may be a while before you find him."

"Why?"

"Many of the Jews taken from Warsaw were shipped to camps hundreds of miles from here. It may take them a good long time to get back home."

"I don't mind waiting," said Rudi. "I've had a lot of practice."

Oscar changed the subject. "Say, why don't you come along with us?"

"Where are you heading?" Rudi asked.

"We stop first at Anna's for a bite to eat—and a little discussion about a particular red wool scarf."

"And then?" asked Rudi.

"Then on to Warsaw," Oscar answered. "We should be there by evening."

"What about them?" said Rudi, pointing toward the German prisoners.

"We'll keep a close watch on them until we get to Warsaw," Oscar said. "I doubt they'll give us any trouble; they're pretty well beaten."

Rudi looked carefully at the prisoners for the first time. None of them could have been older than sixteen.

"They look awfully young," he commented.

"I know. The Germans were getting pretty desperate. Why else would they send boys out to fight a man's war? There's not a one of them who is even old enough to shave yet. If they'd been true soldiers, we wouldn't have captured them, I assure you."

Rudi pretended surprise. "You mean you wouldn't have been able to take them?"

"No!" Oscar shouted. "I mean we'd have shot them. But I don't shoot boys. I'm Polish, not German."

"Well, one thing's sure," said Rudi. "When Anna sees them, she'll feed them a good meal."

Oscar grinned. "You're right, there. Her mother's heart is the only thing that takes precedence over her patriotism."

"And after they've tasted Anna's cooking, you'll have to force them back to Germany," Rudi added.

"Will you join us for some of that cooking?" Oscar asked.

"No, I can't," said Rudi. "I must go straight to Warsaw. But do me a favor, will you?"

"Anything," said Oscar.

"Tell Anna that I'll be back for Ingrid, the little girl I told you about, as soon as I've located my father. You'll remember to tell her that, won't you?"

"I will," said Oscar. "You plan to continue caring for Ingrid even now that the war is over? I'm sure there are those in Warsaw who would care for her. This war's left plenty of children orphans."

"Ingrid won't be going to any orphanage," said Rudi firmly. "She's become like a sister to me; she's not an orphan anymore."

"She's fortunate to have such a brother," said Oscar.

"I think so too," Rudi agreed, striving to part on a cheerful note. "I'll see you soon—if not at Anna's, then in Warsaw." Then he waved good-bye and departed.

As Rudi walked toward the road that led into the city, he thought on the events of the last few years. During that time he had experienced a great many things. He had seen men at their worst—and best—and he knew that what he had seen had changed him forever.

CHAPTER TWENTY-SIX
RETURN TO WARSAW
MAR. 1945

They that dwell under his shadow shall return.
—Hosea 14:7a

What Rudi saw as he entered Warsaw almost made him wish he were back in the forest. The houses and shops were even more decrepit than what he had remembered, and the city was in chaos. The streets were crowded not only with returning Poles but also with Russian, Czech, and Dutch refugees. None of those he passed reminded him of the faces he had once known. Although he desperately needed information, he could not get anyone to even look at him.

He spotted one elderly Polish man and called out to him, "Sir."

The man looked up only for a moment, then hurried on.

"Everybody's so friendly these days," Rudi said irritably.

He then saw a young woman dressed in a white uniform with red sleeve bands. Rudi assumed she was a foreigner. *Maybe it's only the Poles who've lost their manners,* he said to himself, and he determined to see if she could or would speak to him.

"Excuse me," he called.

She stopped and turned toward him.

"I wonder if you could help me," he blurted out before she had a chance to get away.

He was relieved to see her smile. She had understood him, and she did not seem to have any intention of running off.

"If I can," she said. Her Polish was not very good, but Rudi could make out what she was saying. "I'm an American," she continued. "I'm here with the Red Cross. They're sending us all over Europe to help where we can. I must admit, though, I've never been any place where things seemed to be in such a dreadful state of confusion."

"I know what you mean," said Rudi.

"How can I help?" she asked.

"I'm looking for my father."

Her smile faded.

"He was one of the Jews deported by the Germans early in the war," he explained.

She shook her head. "I was hoping you were only going to ask me where you could get a hot meal."

"I can get my own food," said Rudi. "I've been doing that for some time now." Then, fearing he had sounded rather rude, he added, "I suppose you have hundreds of people asking you to help them find their families."

"Thousands, I'm afraid," she said. "But I can take you to the Jewish Relocation Center. They'd be your best source of information."

"I'd really appreciate it," said Rudi.

Her smile returned. She accompanied him to the office building, which was only a few blocks away.

"There it is," she said, stopping. "The office you want is on the third floor."

"Thank you," said Rudi, waving good-bye.

"Hey," she called after him. "What's your name?"

"Rudi," he said. "Rudi Kaplan."

"Well, Rudi," she said, "I hope you find your father."

He smiled as she turned and left. "Thanks again," he called after her.

The Jewish Relocation Center was housed in an old building that had some of the windows blown out. He climbed the worn steps until he came to the right office. It was almost as crowded as the streets. But despite the crowd, there was an oppressive silence in the room, broken only by the droning sound of several aged Jews huddled in one corner, reciting Psalms in Yiddish.

Rudi looked about, trying to decide what to do first. He noticed that some of the people were sitting on the benches waiting, while others stalked the room like caged animals. Still others were standing in a line ending with a man seated at a desk. The line looked to Rudi like the best place to begin.

Once he had taken his place, he turned to see that several people across the room were using pencils, nails, and even pieces of stone to scratch their names onto the stained, cracked wall.

"What are they doing that for?" Rudi asked the man in line behind him.

"It's an act of desperation," said the man. "It's one more way to convince yourself that you're still alive. When you've lost everything, including your family, no one knows—or cares—who you are. You can't even prove that you exist. Take you for instance. What is your name?"

"Rudi Kaplan."

"Prove it."

Rudi was shocked. "What do you mean?"

"You tell me you are Rudi, but I don't know Rudi. You could be lying through your teeth, and I wouldn't

know it. So, rather than believe you, I say you are not
Rudi. It's as simple as that. And you have nothing to
prove otherwise."

"Yes I do," said Rudi defensively. "I have a friend named
Oscar who's coming to Warsaw any day now. I talked
with him only hours ago. And I have a friend who lives
in the village. She knows who I am. And—" He thought
of Ingrid, then remembered that she could tell no one
who he was. "And there are others," he concluded.

"You," the man said quietly, almost bitterly, "are
probably the most fortunate man I've met in days—to
yet have so many friends."

The man then turned from him and spoke no more.

Rudi suddenly felt ashamed for having lashed out at
the man. He tried to think of something comforting to
say. But he could think of nothing, and he was relieved
when he finally heard the man at the desk call out, "Next."

Rudi stepped up. "I'm trying to find my father," he
said.

"Have you checked the list?" the man asked without
looking up.

"What list?"

"Never mind," the man said. "What's your name?"

"Rudi Kaplan."

"Age?"

"Uh, let's see," Rudi paused to calculate. "Sixteen. No,
wait, that's not right. I'm seventeen," he said.

"What's your father's name?"

"Jakob Kaplan."

"When was your father taken?" the man continued.

"At the end of November, 1939," Rudi answered.

For the first time the man at the desk looked up at
Rudi. "I'll be frank with you," he said. "I don't think he
made it if he was taken that long ago."

"I'm not giving up until I'm sure," Rudi said.

The man shrugged.

"How old was he when they took him?"

"Thirty-six," Rudi answered.

"Occupation?"

"He's a doctor," Rudi replied.

The man looked up again. "That's good," he said. "Maybe, just maybe, he made it. Doctors and musicians had a better chance than most," he said as he put the paper aside. "That'll be all. We'll see what we can do."

"Don't you want a description of him or anything?" asked Rudi.

"Descriptions don't seem to do us much good here," the man said. "Nobody looks much the same after the Nazis are done with them."

Rudi started to go, then turned again. "There's one more thing," he said.

The man looked up at him wearily.

"I'd like to find out about the Serdusek family too," he said.

Handing Rudi the typed copy of a list, he said, "Look on there first. If you don't find their name, get back in line. I'll take the information."

Rudi stepped out of line to scan the list. His heart raced as he found the *S*'s. It was there! *Serdusek—101 Nowolipki Street, Apt. #1 (2 occupants).* Rudi stopped. Only two occupants. Who was missing? *Maybe it was just a mistake. Maybe whoever typed the list meant three— not two,* Rudi thought as he handed the list back to the man. "Thank you," he said and headed for the door.

"Hey," Rudi heard someone call after him.

He turned and saw the Jewish man whom he had spoken with in line. "Why don't you write your name up on the wall?" the man said. "Maybe somebody else you know will see it and come looking for you." Although his words seemed harmless, his voice carried a sting.

"No," Rudi said, remembering what the man had said earlier. "Maybe later."

Rudi sensed the man's scornful gaze as he closed the door behind him, and it did little to lighten his spirit. As he walked toward Nowolipki Street, he thought again of the list. What if it were correct? What if only two of the Serduseks had survived? What if Salek had not been as fortunate as he?

Such thoughts continued to plague him even after he had arrived at the Serduseks' door, and it took all the courage he had to reach up and knock.

Mr. Serdusek opened the door slowly. Rudi barely recognized him. He was thin, very thin, and his head had been closely shaved. Also, his expression seemed dull, almost lifeless—until he recognized Rudi. "Rudi!" he cried. It was meant as a shout, but the voice seemed thin and fragile. For a moment, Rudi could not reply.

"Come in! Come in!" Mr. Serdusek urged.

"I tell you, Mr. Serdusek," Rudi managed to say when he had finally found his tongue, "you're the first one in quite some time to recognize me right off. It's a relief to know that I haven't completely changed."

"But you have, son, you have," said Mr. Serdusek.

"Then why was it so easy for you to figure out who I was?" asked Rudi, laughing.

"Because," said Mr. Serdusek, "you're wearing your father's face."

"Have you heard from him?" asked Rudi hopefully.

"Not yet," said Mr. Serdusek. "But we must be patient. The Jews were shipped all over Europe."

"Yes, that's what I've heard," said Rudi.

"It may take him months to get back. And until he does, you will stay with—" Mr. Serdusek stopped a moment, as if remembering some great sorrow. "With us," he eventually managed to say.

Rudi placed his hand on Mr. Serdusek's shoulder, and they stood quietly together. *The list was correct,* thought Rudi.

The thought that he might never see Salek again nearly overwhelmed him, and he banished it from his mind. But it was quickly replaced with thoughts of Mrs. Serdusek, which was no more comforting.

"You want to see Salek, I'm sure," Mr. Serdusek said.

"He is here, then?" Rudi asked, somewhat hesitantly.

"Yes, he is in bed. He's not been well," said Mr. Serdusek. "But he's getting better."

"He'll be all right, won't he?" Rudi asked.

"I think so, but it will take time, Rudi. We have been through—" he stopped, for Salek stood before them.

Rudi could not disguise his shock. Salek's hcad was shaved like his father's. He was not simply thin, however; he was like a skeleton. And he had grown only slightly since he and Rudi had last seen each other. He was dressed in ragged, shabby clothing—castoffs.

"Kind of ugly, aren't I?" Salek said, trying to smile.

"You look better to me right now than you ever looked in all the time we've known each other," Rudi said, walking over to give his friend a hug.

"One thing's sure," said Salek, growing more cheerful. "I haven't had much trouble with my hair sticking up in the back like it used to."

"Come, sit down," Mr. Serdusek said. "You boys can talk while I get us something hot to drink."

"What happened to you, Rudi?" asked Salek. "We thought that they'd taken you at the same time they took your father, but then someone said that you'd escaped. And I must say, you sure don't look like you've paid a visit to the Nazi camps."

"Thanks to my father, I didn't," Rudi said. "He knew they were coming back for him. Your father warned him of that. He made arrangements to have me escape into the forest."

"You mean you've spent over five years in the woods?" asked Salek.

"In the woods and the surrounding villages."

"How in the world did you make it?" asked Salek. "I mean, even I knew more about outdoor life than you did when I last saw you."

"That's true," confessed Rudi, "but I could sure teach you a thing or two now. Really, Salek, when you're better, there's so much I want to show you." And the rest of his words were lost in a rush of emotion.

"A walk in the woods sounds good to me," said Salek. "Maybe in a week or two."

"A month or two," his father added as he entered with the tea. "The boy's a true Serdusek. Never likes to admit that he is ever sick or wrong."

"I seem to remember that," said Rudi, and forced a grin.

"We're doing a lot better, though," said Salek.

"Sometimes," his father teased.

Rudi became serious again. "When were you taken to the work camps?"

"April last year," said Salek.

"We were fortunate to spend only a year in such a place," Mr. Serdusek added.

"But even a few months was too much for mama," said Salek quietly. "I tell you, Rudi, it was awful."

"They took us to Auschwitz," said Mr. Serdusek, turning the conversation specifically from his wife.

"Why did they take you?" asked Rudi.

"There was an uprising in the ghetto."

"So," said Rudi, "the Germans made their Jewish ghetto after all."

"They did," said Mr. Serdusek.

"They crammed all of us into just a few streets," said Salek.

"But I thought that officer, the one in charge—" said Rudi, trying to remember his name.

"Franke?" said Mr. Serdusek.

"Yes, that's the one," said Rudi. "I thought that he might have been able to put a stop to the ghetto order."

"He did, but only for a short time," said Mr. Serdusek.

"It was short, all right," said Salek. "About a month after they had taken the Council members hostage."

"Franke did not stay long," continued Mr. Serdusek. "Apparently, he was a rather decent man. He was military but not a murderer. The Gestapo won the power struggle, and he refused to carry out many of their commands."

"So they sent him back to Germany," Salek said.

"It was then they set up the ghetto. A rebellion was inevitable. But those who fought were half-starved," explained Mr. Serdusek. "The Germans overpowered us."

"When they did, they cleared the ghetto and sent us all off to camps," said Salek.

"I wonder what happened to Franke once he got back to Germany?" asked Rudi.

"I have no idea," said Mr. Serdusek. "But I'll tell you this: even if he lost everything, he was better off than those who continued to do Hitler's work. I do not know how such men could ever sleep at night. Men like Mende."

"I think sleeping is the least of Mende's worries now," said Rudi. "He was one of the German officers killed in the ghetto uprising. I'm sure you had no way of knowing that. I would've hated to be in his place as he stood before God." Then Rudi's thoughts turned to Mrs. Serdusek, and he fell silent.

"I have something that belongs to you," said Mr. Serdusek, rising from his chair.

He left the room and returned only moments later, carrying Dr. Kaplan's Bible.

Rudi took it and held it gently. "How did you get it?" he asked.

"I heard that the Nazis had paid your father a visit," Mr. Serdusek explained. "I went where you had been staying as soon as I'd heard. You know that I was not myself those few days after the interrogation."

"Yes, I remember," said Rudi.

"By the time I got there," Mr. Serdusek said, "you were both gone. I didn't know what to do. I—" he paused before continuing. "It is hard to lose a friend you have known all of your life. I had no assurance that I would ever see him again, and I wanted something, anything from him, you know?"

"I understand," said Rudi. "Believe me, I understand."

"Yes, I think you do," said Mr. Serdusek. "Well, I saw his Bible lying open on the table, and I took it. I—" he could think of no words to express what he was feeling.

"We're Christians now, Rudi," Salek explained. "Mama too."

Rudi could not keep back tears. Yet as he felt them streaming down his face, he knew that they were tears of sorrow as well as joy. He could rejoice in the fact that his and his father's prayers had been answered. All of them would one day be together in heaven. Still, as Rudi looked at his friend, he was again reminded that in this life there is yet much grief. Salek seemed so frail, so tired, so much like he needed his mother by his side. His pain brought to Rudi's mind not only the loss of Mrs. Serdusek but the loss of his own mother also. As the aching loneliness of years returned to him, he found comfort in Christ's words from John 16:33: "These things I have spoken unto you, that in me ye might have peace. In the world ye shall have tribulation: but be of good cheer; I have over-come the world."

Wiping his eyes, he turned again to Mr. Serdusek. "What finally convinced you to believe?" he asked.

"When we were taken away—" He hesitated. Then taking a deep breath, he continued. "We were taken to the camps in cattle cars. Everyone was terrified, for by that time in the war we knew that the camps were not what we had once thought. We knew that only the strongest would be allowed to survive. The old people and young children would be killed.

"On our cattle car there was a man, a Gentile, who began to talk of Christ. Of course, he knew that most of the prisoners were Jews, and at first his conversation angered me. Then I saw that his talk seemed to comfort Sara. One Scripture verse he quoted especially seemed to move her. I'm not certain I could find it now," he said, "but I remember it. It was one your father had quoted to me once. It said, 'He came unto his own and his own received him not. But as many as received him, to them gave He power to become the sons of God.' Sara's whole expression changed when she heard that verse, and though she said nothing, I am certain that at that moment she accepted Christ as her Messiah. I, on the other hand, was still too proud to show the stranger that I was even listening. I—" He had to stop again. "This is very hard for me," he explained.

"I know, " said Rudi. "And you don't have to—"

Mr. Serdusek raised his hand to silence Rudi and continued. "When we arrived at the camp, we were pushed off the train. They were shoving the men and boys to one side, the women and girls to the other. The old people and any children twelve and under were being—taken away, as I said. Salek was fifteen when we were arrested, but he has always been small for his age. When the guards saw him, they shoved him into the line with the children twelve and under. He cried to me, Rudi, but I could do nothing.

"Then behind me I heard my wife cry out, 'Oh, Christ, save my boy.' At that moment another soldier stepped up, grabbed Salek, and threw him back into the line with the other men and boys saying, 'We can still get some work from this one.'

"For the first time, I saw myself for the helpless fool I was. It took Christ to save my boy, the same Christ that I had scorned for years. From that day, Rudi, I have never ceased to call upon Him. Nor will I as long as I live."

"Me either," said Salek softly.

"And I hope someday soon that I can tell this to your father," said Mr. Serdusek.

"I hope so too," Rudi managed to say. "I hope so too."

CHAPTER TWENTY-SEVEN
THE COMING OF MORNING
MAR. 1945

And Jesus . . . delivered him again to his father.
—Luke 9:42b

Rudi was up and out on the streets before dawn. He had left Salek and his father a note, promising them that he would return by evening. He was hoping by that time to have news of his father. Despite everyone's urging for him to be patient, he could not.

Since there was really little he could do at such an early hour, he decided to go and see his old neighborhood and apartment. *Surely the Germans have moved out by now,* he thought.

The city was just beginning to come alive. As he walked, he studied the people who were passing, in the hope of discovering some familiar faces. There were none. Seeing the bakery, the clock shop, and Elias's antique shop caused his mind to flood with memories, but they were memories that now seemed very far away.

The walk from Salek's to his own former home took a lot less time than he had remembered. For that matter, so did getting up to the fourth floor. He now took the stairs three at a time. Reaching his old apartment, he grasped the doorknob and tried to turn it. It was locked. Then he noticed the brass nameplate on the door. The name *Kaplan* had been removed, and a stranger's name was in its place. Slowly he released his hold on the knob and moved toward the stairs. As he did, all the memories of home—and of his father—came back to him, and he sat down on the steps and wept.

Once he had regained his composure, he went out again and spent the next hour or so just walking through the streets. He knew that he had done all he could. Still, it did not seem to be enough, and the longer he walked, the more discouraged and sad he became. He did not want to go to the Serduseks' in a gloomy mood. They had had enough gloom. So he decided to go and see Anna and Ingrid. They would cheer him up, and he could be back to Salek's by dark and in a better frame of mind.

As he walked along the familiar dirt road that led to Anna's, he thought again of the promise he had made to himself to take her flowers when the war had ended. He determined to pick some. The fields were full of wildflowers, and Rudi knew that they were as beautiful as any he had seen in well-kept gardens.

As soon as Rudi entered Anna's cottage, his spirits rose. Ingrid was ecstatic, and Anna as kind as ever.

"I thought you'd like these," he said, handing her the flowers.

"They're beautiful, Rudi," she said. "Just beautiful."

She motioned for him to sit down while she went to get a vase for the flowers. As he did so, he took Ingrid on his knee.

"I brought you something too," he said to her, taking several smooth stones from his pocket.

By the time Anna returned, Ingrid was sitting and happily drawing at the table with Rudi.

"I wonder how old she is?" Rudi asked.

"Nine, I believe."

"She doesn't look nine."

"Still, she acts about that age," Anna replied. "It's true she's small, but she learns quickly. And you know how well she can draw. Maybe her parents were small."

"Maybe," said Rudi. Then he smiled. "If she has to be small, at least she's a girl."

"Size doesn't much matter in girls or boys," said Anna in her motherly tone.

Rudi nodded. "That's true. Salek's short—and awful skinny, now—but he's still a great friend."

Anna turned. "You found him, then!" she exclaimed.

"I did," said Rudi. "He and his father are back in Warsaw."

"And his mother?" asked Anna.

Rudi shook his head and glanced down.

"I'm sorry," she said.

"There is one good thing," said Rudi. "She had never believed in Christ. But before she died, she did. She turned to Him for salvation."

Rudi saw that Anna was carefully taking in what he had to say. He was glad of it. Although Anna believed in God, Rudi feared that her beliefs encouraged her to trust in her own goodness. He feared that like so many others in his country, she had not yet recognized her need to depend solely on Christ for salvation.

"My father and I had prayed for them for years," Rudi continued, "but they had never believed. Mr. Serdusek was especially antagonistic. He was a leader in the Jewish community. But right before my father was taken, Mr. Serdusek seemed to soften. Then, when they were deported, another prisoner again spoke to them of Christ."

Rudi related the entire incident to Anna just as Mr. Serdusek had told it to him. When he finished, he could tell that she was genuinely moved. He waited for her to speak. When she did not, he decided to continue.

"You know," he went on, "I have known Christ since I was very young. But these past few days I've come to understand more of His love than I've ever known before. We both knew that this war was brutal, but I had no idea how brutal until I went back into the city. When I returned to Warsaw, I realized how good God has been to me. I never told you of my father's promise, did I?"

"No," said Anna. She was still listening intently.

"When my father discovered that he was to be deported, he prayed for guidance about what he should do with me. God gave him a promise that if he let me go, I would live to see the end of the war. The verse that assured him of my safety was Psalm 91:1: "He that dwelleth in the secret place of the most High shall abide under the shadow of the Almighty.""

"I have read that," she said.

"I had too, many times," said Rudi. "Still, I wasn't ready to believe it. I remember my father saying, 'The forest is God's secret place for you, Rudi. There—there you shall be under His shadow where you will be safe.' It seemed so unreasonable then, but now I've seen those who come from the camps. They're no more than walking skeletons, and they seem so bewildered and helpless. God not only kept me alive, but He also made me healthy and strong."

"And your father," she asked hesitantly, "did he have such a promise concerning his own safety?"

"No," said Rudi quietly. "But I still believe that the same God who kept me under His shadow could have kept my father as well. And I will keep that faith until God shows me otherwise."

"I admire you—and your faith," she said.

Rudi felt that he had said enough for the moment, but he determined that he would talk to her on the subject again.

"Can Ingrid stay here with you until I do locate my father?" he asked her.

"She can stay with me as long as you will let her," Anna said.

"Good. By the way, has Josef come back?" asked Rudi.

"Only for his things," said Anna. "He said he was going to Germany where he can be free."

Rudi shook his head.

"I wonder if Oscar's right about him," she said. "Maybe he is past hope."

"You mustn't say that," said Rudi. "It makes me furious to remember how rude and unkind he's been to you. But even so, I know you, and I know you won't give up on him. You love him, though I must admit it's hard for me to see why."

"Maybe it's because he is named for my husband," she said. "And he is family. You love your family. I just can't give up hope on those I love."

"I understand, and you're right," he said. "How about Oscar? Have you seen much of him?"

"Not since he brought your message to me. I thought you might have seen him in Warsaw."

"Not yet," said Rudi. "I intend to, though. I want to thank him for what he did for me and also to tell him of my father's promise as I told you. I think it would do him good to hear how God used him."

"I don't think he'll be eager to give God the credit for your survival," said Anna.

"I didn't say he'd like hearing it; I just said it would do him good," Rudi said, smiling. "I should have told him right from the start, but he frightened me a bit when I first knew him. He has a rough exterior."

"True," said Anna. "But you mustn't think that you have failed him. He knew your father's reputation, and he knew what your father believed. Your willingness to learn from him and your courage says a great deal to a man like Oscar."

"I hope so."

"What exactly have you done toward finding your father?"

"I've registered with the Jewish Relocation Center," he said. "And I've looked through the city for him."

"And now?" she asked.

Rudi shrugged. "I don't know."

"I think you do."

"What are you suggesting?"

"I'm suggesting that you not only *believe* as your father believes but that you also *do* what your father would do," she said.

Rudi looked puzzled.

"Once he'd done all that he could to find you," Anna continued, "do you think he would sit around waiting for you or spend his time walking aimlessly through the streets looking for you?"

"No, I guess he wouldn't," Rudi admitted.

"What would he do, then?" she asked him.

He thought a moment. "I suppose he would do what he could to help the people around him."

"Exactly," she said. "You're the one who said that there are hundreds in the city who need help."

"My father is a doctor, Anna. I'm not. What can I do?"

"Think, Rudi, of all that you have learned these past years. You know how to cook. You could help feed people. You've learned how to work with your hands. The houses and buildings in the city certainly could use repair. You told me that you helped your father for several months. You could even work in a hospital, if you had a mind to."

"Anna," he said, getting up to leave, "I think you and my father would get along very well." He bent down and kissed her cheek. Then, turning to Ingrid, he said, "I'll be back later this week, and I'll bring you a fresh supply of stones."

As he went out, Sasha met him in the dooryard. She leaped against his legs and licked his hands. He was glad to see her, too, but as soon as Ingrid came to the doorway to wave good-bye, Sasha instantly darted away to join her.

It was late in the afternoon by the time Rudi again reached Warsaw. On his way to the Serduseks', he again passed the building that housed the Jewish Relocation Office. People were still streaming in and out of it. He stopped and thought a moment. *It can't hurt,* he said to himself as he started up the stairs.

"Excuse me," he said to one man as he entered the room. "Do you have something I could write with?"

The man did not bother to reply but pointed toward a woman who had just finished writing her name.

"Ma'am," said Rudi coming up behind her, "may I borrow that a moment?"

She gave him the worn, chalk-like stone without comment and walked away.

He sighed deeply, and again his heart grew heavy with the sadness of those around him. Anna certainly had a point: he had no right to waste time moping with so many people all around him who were in need. With new resolve, he raised his hand and wrote boldly on the wall: *Rudi Kaplan is alive. Psalm 91:1*

"Of course he is," a man behind him said. "And he has grown as well."

Rudi stopped, afraid for a moment to turn around, afraid that he would find a stranger. But then he felt a hand upon his shoulder. He turned. It was no stranger.

"Papa," he said, almost in a whisper.

Although his father was as thin and gaunt as others who had suffered in the Nazi camps, there was yet laughter in his eyes as he reached out to touch Rudi's cheek. "Still no beard," he said, smiling.

Rudi took his father in his arms. "Ah, papa," he said, holding him close, "I now have your stature and mother's wit. I do not need a beard."

EPILOGUE

But your eyes have seen all the great acts of the Lord which he did. Therefore shall ye keep all the command- ments which I command you this day, that ye may be strong.
—Deuteronomy 11: 7-8a

Shortly after Poland's liberation the country was again enslaved, this time by the chains of communism. The Yalta agreement, which ended the war in Europe, placed Poland under Russia's jurisdiction. Stalin, Russia's leader, was to offer "protection" to the Poles until their government could be reestablished. It was soon evident, however, that Stalin intended to dominate rather than protect the Polish people.

Jakob Kaplan and Eryk Serdusek were quick to discern the similarities between Stalin's and Hitler's political ambitions. Fearing further persecution, the men fled with their families to Stockholm, Sweden, before Stalin's Communist regime could become firmly entrenched.

Once in Sweden, Rudi and Salek were able to complete their high school education and enter the same university their fathers had attended. Rudi studied medicine; Salek, law. Under Dr. Kaplan's care, Ingrid again learned to speak. Rudi also convinced her to exchange her drawing stones and bark pencils for paint and canvas, and eventually she became an accomplished artist.

249

Life in Sweden did much to heal the painful memories of the war years. There was, however, one important truth that the Kaplans and Serduseks had been taught through their suffering, one truth that they would never forget: nothing could separate them from the love of Christ. Despite tribulation, distress, famine, peril, and sword, God had allowed them all to emerge as conquerors. And He had enabled Rudi to travel a road that took him beyond his boyhood dreams of heroism to a life of true courage.

1. *The modern-day trumpeter of Krakow*

2. (inset) *The statue of King Sigmund at the naval castle in Warsaw*
3. *The naval castle in Warsaw*

4. *Warsaw before the destruction*

5. *Warsaw after the destruction*

6. *German Ju.87 Stuka dive-bombers*

7. *An air-raid shelter constructed at a marketplace*

8. *Posting regulations for the Jews*

9. *Burning Jewish property in a marketplace*

10. *A deportation from the Warsaw ghetto*

11. *The destruction of Warsaw*

12. and 13. *The deportation from the Warsaw ghetto*

Map of
The German
Invasion of Poland
Fall 1939

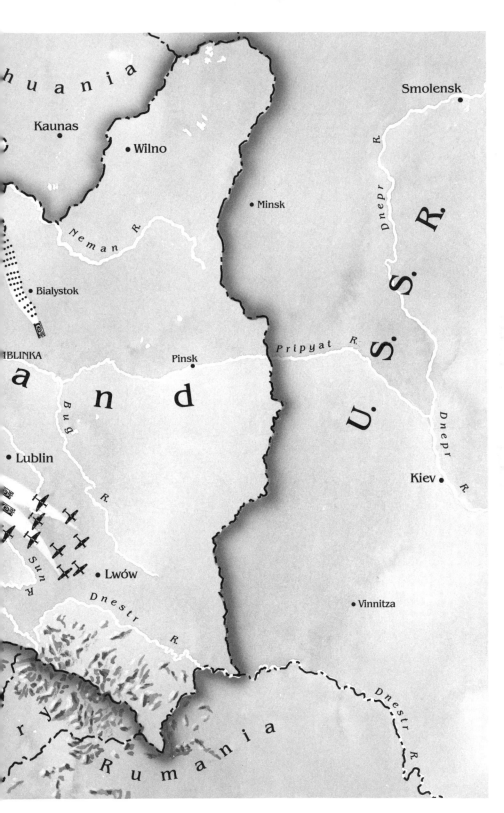